AND THAT WAS THE MOMENT THAT THE SHIELD FAILED ...

The human crew of *Discovery* had been trained for just such an instance, and knew exactly what to do. No discussions were held – each crew member had one specific area of responsibility and knew exactly what to do in that area in order to save the situation.

And if there was ever a situation that needed saving, it was this one... If nothing was done, the ship would literally melt from the inside out, and if the machinery of the shield was destroyed as a result, then the crew would be exposed to the storm without shielding....

CONTINGENCIES

THOMAS WHITE

Ocean Beach Books
San Francisco

Copyright © 2011 Thomas White. All rights reserved.

Published by Ocean Beach Books, a division of Ocean Beach Kft.
LLC, 5758 Geary Boulevard, San Francisco, CA 94121 USA

ISBN 978-0-615-54535-6

Printed in the United States of America
First printing 2011

To Dragon

ACKNOWLEDGMENTS

To Carey and Eszter and Alex, because they are awesome. To Halo and Mass Effect and Larry Niven and Orson Scott Card and Arthur C. Clarke and Isaac Asimov and Neal Stephenson and Michio Kaku because they are awesome as well, though perhaps not as much so as Eszter and Carey and Alex. And to Mr. Reid, who read my entire thing in 6th grade, even though he probably had much better and more interesting things to do at the time. Finally, to my computer, which underwent a relentless beating for an incomprehensible period of time yet remains reliable and effective.

They are all staring. All of them.

The corridor is dark, blank, as is fitting for an underground bunker. I could possibly touch both walls simultaneously, were it not for the fists, seemingly of iron, which dig into my wrists. Their movements are automatic, quick and robotic; they react to nothing I do.

All of those eyes are boring into me.

My Engineer's uniform clings dryly to my skin. It is sweaty and dirty, yet all the more obvious for it.

They line the walls, an unending carpet of the last few who remain faithful to Him. Their ME-C suits, a technology that might have won the War three decades ago, are pathetic hints of what could have been. All of those red visors. Staring at me.

They know I was one of them. *Think* I was one of them. My uniform reveals all. I wonder: *How many of these were at Waterfront? How many of them were there in the Town Hall that night?*

As we come to the corridor's end, everything shakes. Little flakes of concrete and plasteel fall from the roof. The U.C. is closing in now; they'll be in the city soon. The shield will hold them off for a while. If only… But no.

The guards who stand at the corridor's end eye me with a palpable air of distain. I am a insect, a traitor; something not worthy of their attention or worry. The small, standard-issue gun at my side is regarded with amusement; after all, the shields they are dealing with have withstood nuclear weapons.

One of them waves me lazily in, barely glancing up from his task of looking as dangerous as possible.

There is another rumble, as the U.C. reach the missile silos that unleashed nuclear death on them, one day long ago.

The approach to it is carefully monitored. To describe it as a door would be to capture only a small fraction of its majesty. It is massive, monolithic; plasteel and carbon nanotube flash blindingly as it lumbers open. I can see that it is at least three feet thick – large enough to withstand nuclear missiles, even without the help of the shields that are undoubtedly present.

We step through; my guards exit mechanically and efficiently. The door closes behind us with a thud that is ominously final.

I get closer. There are lights on in the hall. Voices, though few.

The room is larger, significantly. A small circle on the floor marks the boundaries of the energy shield that separates me from the others. The thin blue line…There are three in total – the lone guard on the right is one, the aide another. And then there is the third.

Closer, closer. The speech is rare, from only a few voices. My stomach curls in fear.

He sits there on the chair, a simple military uniform hanging loosely. One more pathetic reminder.

This man launched the first great nuclear war. This man fought and demolished and destroyed for the next sixty years. This is the man who put down the Waterfront Revolution.

The aide is speaking. After a considerable pause, my brain registers them.

"…found her trying to deactivate the shields of the city. She had done some damage, but we caught her. Your verdict?"

Someone says something, the hysteria rising on their tongue.

He says nothing for a second.

"What did she manage to damage?"

The aide replies over the course of several seconds, obviously speaking to someone else over a something in his ear.

"We are not sure yet, but most of the damage was caused to the shields inside the city…"

There is a single, beautiful, frozen moment as he realizes the meaning of this fact. Understanding dawns on three faces. The Sanctum shields are part of the city's network. They are connected in the same router as the city shield, which I didn't manage to disable. And that thin blue line on the floor, the line which was supposed to protect them against anything I could do, means absolutely nothing at all.

The men bark an order…

All those years in the Home Guard, and the years afterwards, have trained me well. One shot is heading towards its target before the pistol is even out of my hoister. The second, similarly accurate, hits the aide in the temple. Then I stop.

The man sitting across from me, the one who started the greatest war humankind has ever known, is silent. Weary. As if what he had to realized for the last few years is dawning, finally, upon him. The War is over.

Slowly, gracefully, the shots ring out. One by one. Continuously. For longer than I can comprehend. Again and again and again. Soldiers of the Union must not waste ammunition, for fear of endangering the war effort. And then, the Town Hall is totally, completely silent.

I fire.

1

David R. Wu started out of a window.

Perhaps a twentieth-century observer might have found his name strange; in his time it was not something that anyone would have noticed.

This is not to say that a twentieth century observer might not be comfortable with him – in every way he was average and that was something that had not changed overly throughout the centuries. His hair was dark, with a hint of blond, his eyes were bluish, and he was of average height, build and stature. In fact, generally the only reason that anyone might comment on his appearance would be to single him out as a shining example of averageness.

There was only a single feature of him that could possibly have been notable, and that was one that no one of his century would have commented on. His limbs were long, unnaturally so, making him both several inches taller and a significant fraction frailer than a human had any right to be.

At the moment, though, the person in question was not thinking about any of these things. Instead, he was looking out of the window.

It was an irritatingly small widow, barely four inches square. David, of course, knew that this size was necessary to maintain its strength – had the window been larger, say, then David would have been at a significant risk of dying in a vacuum, a fate that he had learned a great deal about in his former home.

However, despite all logic and explanation, the window was annoyingly small.

Outside, though, Earth was beautiful. The clouds were plentiful, and only a few traces of electrically lighted continent were visible. They obscured well the suffering and reconstruction that still pervaded ten years after the War. Perhaps it was better this way – David had seen enough of that in the last ten years, and just now he was not willing to see any more.

Earth was a sight that he knew well. Every night of his childhood, for about as long as he could remember, he had spent much of every night watching it. Sitting in his bed, staring out of the Dome, he had watched the flash of Orbital Ion Cannons, the twinkle of nuclear weapons, and tried to push back the ever-present thought: *Will we be all that's left?*

This was a problem that was in everybody's minds. Because of international colonization of the moon, the opinions on the war were numerous and varied. Were it not for their location, perhaps war would have broken out. However, in a place where everyone was in constant danger and the slightest crack could spell disaster, conflict was simply not possible, and everybody knew it well

Perhaps they could be excused for this constant brooding. Every lunar day, the spacecraft *Endurance* arrived at the unnecessarily named "Launch Pad One", and everyone, regardless of political affiliation, went to greet it.

David later suspected that they were starved for news of Earth, regardless of the context or source.

What came out was its own reward. The United Countries, incapable of evacuating their people from the invasion, had chosen to do the next best thing. Every aspect of their culture and history was sent, carefully, watchfully, away from the destruction and battle to somewhere where it would be safe. At the time, of course, David knew none of this. But he knew what it meant.

The ship would slowly dock, open and prepare. Then, the treasures would come out. Some of them David knew well, so well that merely being in their presence was a reward. "Starry Night", an original signed version of the European Confederation, Apollo 13, the Rosetta Stone – all were treated as artifacts of incredible power. There were those that he knew little of, but researched of and learned about afterwards – Samurai armor, the British Crown Jewels, a great jade statue of the Buddha. Then, there were those that he had never learned of or even heard about. He struggled for details to discover their purpose – a scroll of unknown purpose that seemed Chinese, an ancient-looking paper labeled, in massive letters, *We The People*, and, most important to him, an enigmatic picture of a smiling woman. He had seen it for only a few seconds before it was pulled away by the *Endurance*'s crew, but it had left a lasting image on his mind for years. The people had said that it had been evacuated from France only minutes before the place it had been stored in was destroyed. For years afterwards, David had wondered what she was smiling about.

Even the treasures, amazing as they were, were not enough for David's young mind. Perhaps they were not enough for anyone. For after the valuables were moved and stored with infinite care, the colony did not leave. The ship's crew, always different, was welcomed, fed and housed, even if just for a few hours. In return, the crew told stories.

This was the part that David, and indeed much of the colony, enjoyed above all else. For hours, they would sit and listen, for hours on end, about the Third Battle of Stalingrad, the loss of Washington, the slow push through Tokyo, the sustained guerilla battles in Jerusalem, Iraq, Australia and London. The stories, often firsthand, of the war were latched on to by everyone as their only source of news besides the sometimes difficult to trust radio transmissions they received from both sides. But they held a special fascination for David. He grew up on a war that was just on his doorstep, but impossible to reach. A war that was infinitely glorified by his child's mind. A war that was the epitome of what he wanted to do.

So he listened to stories, eagerly, every time he could. He heard of the Second Battle of Washington, the ventures into Canada, the slow, one-sided battle as the United Countries was pushed slowly back into its land. Then, one day, he heard of the Battle of Port City, Alaska, and Operation PHOENIX, the moment where the historians of the future would place the thin red line labeled "The Turning Point."

For the next thirty years, the United Countries pushed the South African Union back through China and Brazil and Cuba and Cairo and Bagdad, and for thirty more years the Endurance, still the only ship with a Pandemonium shield, came. No longer bringing treasures, of course, for the U.C.'s territory was now safe from war. Instead, they brought wine, ice cream, superconductor, aluminum, all the things that the moon did not have and the U.C. could now spare.

Still, David kept the dream of the War alive, at least inside himself, keeping it even into his adulthood.

As all things come to an end, so the War eventually ground to a halt. The United Countries slowly closed in on Capitol City; the Dictator of South African was shot by his allies. The sun went back to a normal radiating level, and humankind looked back towards the Stars.

David had wasted almost no time – he had traveled to Earth to help with the cleaning up of a war that he had barely missed. He worked there for eight years.

Those eight years were the worst of his life. For eight years David had tried to rebuild cities, communities, families. For eight years he saw not the side of the war that he was supposed to – not the heroic fight to defeat an irrational enemy – but the legacy that every war has. He saw the ruined houses, the nuclear wastelands, the destroyed cities.

He had tried to help. He had made it his mission to fix as many problems as he could come in contact with. He worked hard for eight years to fix what the War had caused. Then he had stopped. Perhaps he was frustrated with the lack of affect that the recovery efforts were having. Perhaps he was simply tired. But for whatever reason, (as he was unsure himself), he had joined the mission.

The shuttle shifted under him, breaking David's brooding. He squeezed his eyes shut, hand on his forehead, and then looked up.

The corporations that produced shuttles designed them to have in-factors of one hundred. Because of this, the shuttle was entirely full. It was a commercial shuttle, most probably borrowed for a song from Delta-American. The Space Administration had gotten it free, which would please the taxpayers. On the other hand, it was also a commercial shuttle, with all the attributes that that implied. Definitely not the most dignified mode of travel for a mission of this importance.

Partially because of his lack of room, David craned his neck to view the cabin. There was some talk, of course, as is liable to happen if one hundred human beings are placed into a small room. Overall, though, the cabin was remarkably quiet. Perhaps, as with David, the reality of the mission was slowly, yet unstoppably sinking in.

With amusement David noticed that Ian and James were seated as far away from each other as the relatively small volume of the cabin would allow. Ian Whitcomb was a brilliant astrobiologist and computer scientist, and was an excellent choice for the mission. James Ackerson was equally well qualified as a geologist and astronomer. Both had

5

received Nobel Prizes: both were counted as some of the greatest minds in their generation. David could easily see the motivation in bringing one of them. Bringing both, in his opinion, was both dangerous and foolhardy.

In a rivalry that stretched back to the 2141 Astrobiology conference in Geneva, the two men had gone from political enemies to personal ones. Although neither was particularly murderous, bets were going on how long one of them would last. In David's personal opinion, they would last a few weeks in the close confines of a spaceship. By most, his opinion was seen as conservative.

Most likely, their personal and scientific passion outweighed the difficulty of having people they hated along. What was perhaps most interesting about the mission, though was that this was not the predominant motivation for being aboard.

Juliana Walters, seated two rows ahead of him (her darkish brown hair being the only easy notification, given the close confines), was a perfect example. She had been born in Capital City in the waning days of the war, and, although she had originally been a patriot of the South African cause, she became one of the few living witnesses of the striking down of the Waterfront Revolution. Rapidly losing faith in the South African leader's judgment and sense of morality, she had conceived a plan to end the South African cause. Over the next two years, she had worked her way up the ranks, eventually becoming a chief engineer of the city's Pandemonium shield. By the time she achieved this; the United Countries was rapidly closing in, already only a few miles from the city. She had, in a desperate move, attempted to shut down the city's shield network, leaving it defenseless. Shields in the city were effectively neutralized, but she was caught before her main objective, the exterior shield, was destroyed.

She was taken directly before the Dictator, whose state of mental health was rapidly declining at the time. However, she was not deprived of her general-issue sidearm. The assumption was that she could do no harm with it. After all, there was a protective shield between her and the Dictator.

Perhaps unfortunately, the Home Guard had failed to check how much damage she had caused and to what.

In a single shot, Juliana Walters made herself into a hero in a good portion of the world's mind and an antithesis of virtue the minds of the remainder. For eight years she was one of the most controversial figures in the Earth-Moon system. For eight years the United Countries had found it necessary to place a guard over her; for eight years she was analyzed like a specimen. Thus, her motivation was in no way in question. It was true, of course that they would continue to be contact with Earth throughout the mission. But, as a great deal of exploration had proven, a few million miles was always a good buffer from society.

David knew that such distancing was a major motivation of the crew, though no one said so out loud. Personally, David did not know. All that he knew was that he had to leave had to get away from something that towered over him on Earth. He had to get away from …

Then he stopped. With a sigh, he decided that the question was only causing him anxiety – something that was not entirely appreciated in the current environment. He momentarily kneaded his nose with his fingers, stretched his neck, and then decided that the window would provide the necessary ample distraction.

The shuttle was slowly curving away from Earth, which no longer filled the entire view. Slowly, more and more human artifacts came into view.

Apparent and powerful was the sharp glow of a Power Satellite's shield absorbing energy. With a slight shock, David realized that the satellite was one of the original Power Satellites from the great 2040 effort. It must be nearly a century old now. A century of running nearly an entire continent. And the U.C. still could not replace it. The rebuilding effort had taken its toll in costs as well as time.

In front of it was the characteristic tapered cone shape of an Orbital Ion Cannon, still vigilant even in this time of peace. Despite their victory, the United Countries had failed to take them down for the last decade, and many suspected that it would never be done. Perhaps a victim of bureaucratic process, the Ion Cannon was still ready, a watchful sentry, and would for a long time be ready for war, even if no war existed.

With a gravitational tilt, the shuttle turned, and finally David noticed Spacedock, which in many ways was unique. It was, of course, the system's largest space station, at nearly five miles across. It occupied the fifth (and most stable) Lagrangian point between the Earth and Moon. But, by far the most irritatingly to the United Countries Space Administration, they did not own it. In fact, it was a private corporation, rudely shattering the national space exploration myth that had fueled the space race of the twentieth century. Of course, they were not the first – NASA had relied on private companies based in the Mojave desert for lifting since 2015, and indeed a great deal of the space industry's cash flow had historically been corporation-based. That was not the problem. The problem was that Spacedock held a complete monopoly on spaceship production. Worse, not only did they know it, they positively rejoiced in it. Occupying the only economical spot for a spaceship production facility of the necessary size in the Earth-Moon system, they could charge incredible prices with no resistance whatsoever. When confronted about this fact, their answer was inevitably the same: "You *do* want a ship built, right?"

The Space Administration had struggled for years with the simple fact that the only way to build a spaceship in orbit was to pay someone else. The truth was, unfortunately, that there was very little that they could do short of sending in the Marines. Many, many attempts to dislodge Spacedock's monopoly had been made throughout the decade. However, this time, David's mission might actually work, and Spacedock knew it too.

Regardless of the possible impending destruction of their business, Spacedock, for the moment at least, was doing fine. As they passed, David spent several minutes simply taking in the detail of tens on ships of every size and shape slowly coming together. Passenger airliners took shape next to cargo freighters of all models. David, however, was far more familiar with one particular category – the solar sail-powered sports yachts. There were several, including a smaller Photon type, several Gale-models, and even a Firefly model, a carbon copy of David's own. He eyed them appreciatively with a practiced eye.

Solar sailing had been one of his few distractions during his years as an ambassador. The ships were usually tiny, but that was almost attractive. Most important, by far, though, was simply the stillness and slow pace of the sport.

He would sit in the cabin for hours, making a pull on the lines that controlled the massive, nearly half a kilometer square sail. The incredibly thin sail, a few molecules across, was just thin enough to make economical the use of one of the great energy sources of the Solar System. The sun acted as a massive producer of electromagnetic waves, of course, but it also emitted countless particles. On half a square kilometer of sail, they created as much pressure as the landing of a grasshopper. *But it would keep creating that same pressure indefinitely.* As long as the sail was oriented correctly to the solar wind, that pressure would keep coming when a rocket's fuel might run out after a few minutes. However, a solar sailship could never rise from the surface, where it could not even collect the necessary thrust. Only in space were they effective.

This left David's job much as an ancient mariner's he would keep the sail oriented, facing the correct direction, and in one piece. This was one of the principal points of his job. If the sail became unstable or started to ripple, it incredibly thin molecular fabric would tear itself apart. And there was no replacing half a square kilometer of sail.

He had been, and still was, an expert, winning the Gyro-Moon competition five times. This skill was entirely secondary to being an ambassador, of course. However, it had done something that his major job hadn't done: it had gotten him a place on the mission.

The spacecraft *Discovery* had a sail as well; a sail that was nearly seven kilometers across. This was necessary to propel the ship's vast bulk, of course, but it also amounted to one of the most daunting challenges of David's career. Only two members of *Discovery*'s crew would be assigned to fourteen square kilometers of carbon nanotube weave.

The shuttle crested the main, wheel-shaped section of Spacedock, and then David saw *Discovery* for the first time.

Of course, he had participated in countless simulations and practice sessions and knew his way around the ship like the proverbial back of his hand. He knew what everything did, and in a state of emergency could function as a shield mechanic or computer technician, though it would take a very significant emergency to make him try it. But somehow, inexplicably, all of that had somehow failed to communicate the true size of *Discovery*. Only then, as he saw it for himself, did it finally settle in that the ship was nearly a cubic kilometer.

Discovery was a cylinder rotating around a central axis. The resulting centrifugal force created an approximation of gravity on the inner surface, which was divided itself into rotating compartments that would also be livable if the ship was not rotating. These compartments held crew quarters, storage that had to be kept under gravity, and the farms, which provided oxygen, some food and a very significant morale boost. The inner axis, meanwhile, held much of the ship's machinery, including the A.I. core, Pandemonium shield and sail controls.

The though suddenly occurred to David that, had the sail not been there, he would still probably be on Earth. The thought that he was not caused him to be momentarily very happy, and then extremely confused afterwards. Why had he thought that?

Whatever the reason, the monolithic creations of Man did not wait for him to finish thinking. With a great, metallic clang, the shuttle docked with Discovery.

"They've launched the mission successfully."

"Can you believe what they called the ship?"

"What?"

"Discovery."

"Oh, the irony... did you set that up?"

"No – absolute coincidence."

"Now that is a surprise."

"Regardless, we are one hundred percent on schedule."

"Good. In a matter of this delicacy, one must take everything one can get."

2

Discovery's Algorithmically Deductive Administrative Mainframe was bored.

This situation was significantly more annoying than it might have been in a human. There were several reasons for this: ADAM had a far greater processing power than such a human, but had, at least at this point, comparatively less to do.

The last was perhaps most surprising, given that he was presiding over the launching of a spacecraft. The amount of tasks to be preformed was astronomical. However, ADAM's subroutines were handling it quite effectively, requiring no interference from his sentient mind. Furthermore, had he been forced to carry out these tasks himself, he would most probably been more bored then he was now, although in a different and admittedly unique way.

There was, of course, an equally astronomical amount of information that he could have spent time absorbing.

However, this type of activity, and many like it, was disqualified for one very significant reason: the significance of the situation, both for ADAM himself and for the human race, was far above frivolous activities like typing random phrases into search engines and then starting to read. Indeed, this fact left the amount of activities that he could perform annoyingly low.

The solution that had been historically used was to say something grave and historic to a crewmember. Actually, it mattered very little what it was, but something was rather necessary. Unfortunately for ADAM, the entire human component of *Discovery* was chemically knocked out for acceleration that was soon to endure. This left ADAM with no one to talk to besides the hundreds of media groups carefully scrutinizing every aspect of the mission, and he was not particularly enthusiastic about any more of talking to them then he absolutely had to.

ADAM pondered the quandary for several minutes with no success. Eventually, he decided that an inspection of the ship, despite the fact that it was both remarkably orthodox and equally pointless, would still serve to cure (at least momentarily), his boredom.

It was true to say that *Discovery* was a marvel. Actually, it held this status for two reasons. The ship was incredibly advanced, with technology not available outside the government and above-military grade hardware. Perhaps more incredibly, though, it cost nearly eight billion Units of taxpayer money. ADAM had not met many politicians in his thus far relatively short life, but those he had did not seem willing to spend eight billion on the space program.

Yet, somehow, *Discovery* stubbornly continued existing. Each component, incredibly advanced, did too. ADAM spent only a few minutes looking around before realizing that there were some areas and objects that even he hadn't been told about. A server stack in the Computation area, a series of instruments near the front of the hull, a progressively thinner, cone-shaped set of conduits running from the front to the rear of the ship; all these things ADAM had not been even told the purpose of. Someone knew, of course, but his role was simply not specialized enough for these things.

Unfortunately, the ship was of limited size, and there came a point where he simply could examine it no more. However, the activity had served its purpose. By the time he was finished, the tanker was drifting away; tugs, like minnows next to a whale, were pushing Discovery away from Spacedock. Two fusion thrusters were slowly attached, and then everything, human or not, cleared the area.

The initiative was all ADAM's. For a few seconds, he merely contemplated on the situation. Eventually, though, it seemed the period allocated for a solemn pause was over, and people were beginning to feel impatient. He paused for a few seconds anyway, and then sent a simple command down a fiber optic cable. The command was accepted, and a series of actions were taken.

A cone of fusion fire emerged from *Discovery*'s rear, and the first mission to Mars began.

3

David woke up, and he was home. He sat in his bed, in the apartments of Plato City, and contemplated getting up. Eventually, he succeeded. *Damn it. The eight o'clock rain has started. I need to get down there before…*

His head smashed into the low ceiling. Crying out, he sat back on the bed, heavily, then looked around.

In the place of his window onto the Plato City Dome, there was a blank stretch of functional, slightly grayish wall. Slowly, it dawned on him that his apartment was receding at a speed that had rarely been achieved before. Adjusting for a heavier gravity then at home, he made another attempt at standing up.

This was when he smashed his head for the second time in the day.

Nevertheless, his second attempt was in most ways a success, as he had succeeded in standing up. It was then that the fact finally worked its way into his brain: that the

15

centrifuge was still spinning up, and it had reached only the point of lunar gravity.

The illusion had been remarkable, though. All of a sudden, David felt the habits of a third of a century come rushing back all at once. He pushed against his bedpost, clipped the room's small desk with his fingernail, and sent himself slowly arching towards the room's door.

Outside, he glanced momentarily down the long, equally grayish corridor (the holopanels not yet having been set) before directing his attention to Jacob's door, which was in the process of sliding open.

The man who emerged was tall and wiry, but very obviously strong. His face somehow managed to look concerned, thoughtful, and powerful all at once. Because of his position as the other solar sail mechanic on the ship, David knew him well. He was far less dangerous then he looked, certainly, although he was certainly one of powerful wit. Given his sudden exit, David felt himself rather flustered, and so it was after nearly a second that he responded with the not particularly eloquent, "Sleep well?"

"No, actually. This thundering kept me up. It was like someone had switched a frakking fusion drive on."

The sarcasm was palpable, but nevertheless funny.

"I got some pretty good knockout drops. Didn't Mission Control force some into your mouth?"

"Oh, you mean the cough drops? I think I ate those during the mission briefing. Certainly made it more interesting, though. Sorry."

David groaned. The jokes were bad, as was expected after such a sudden waking.

"How many people do you think are awake?"

"Probably not many. I think we're rather early."

"...So?"

"Let's go."

The pair began walking down the corridor, towards an equally grayish doorway, Jacob moving considerably less gracefully then David. Past that was another, which led them into the central series of corridors running through the ship. They rounded a corner, reached another door, and waited for it to open.

The holographic sunlight that emerged was blinding. With eyes adjusted to dull electric light, it took David several, quite painful, seconds to adjust.

When they did, he found himself staring at the perfect, clear blue of sky. It faded downwards, mixing slowly with the green of land, until it reached the actual floor.

Perhaps floor was a bad word to describe it – for the ground was covered in dirt and water, populated by endless types of trees. There was an English garden to his left, a near jungle beyond that. In every way the illusion was incredibly powerful – a soft breeze ruffled his hair, and the chirps of birds filled the air. Vivid was a clear, summery smell.

There were some outposts of artifact in the sea of green. The first was a pavilion was in the center, placed there by the sociologists for purposes of "group binding". The second was a series of small huts along the sides of the centrifuge, looking, above their plasteel interiors, every bit as if they had been erected by some primitive tribe. When one entered them, however, they shed immediately this humble appearance. Inside were games, table tennis, lounges, reading rooms, and countless other devices for bored crew members. There was, of course, the Simroom, and there was the shooting range.

However, their destination was the third, which consisted of a great, long, careful artfully carved mahogany table, massively out of place inside a jungle. As they approached it, David realized that they had been not among the first to arrive, but the last. The table's one hundred seats were nearly full, as the voyage's first breakfast was consumed.

David walked over to a humble metal device to the right of the table, then spoke, enunciating carefully," Earl Grey with sugar, three strips of bacon with waffles and butter." He then returned to the table, found a seat next to

Arkady Bogdanov, Pandemonium shield mechanic and former member of the South African Home Guard, and sat as his food was delivered efficiently and robotically.

It was only then that he noticed that the table was totally silent. Realizing this, though not quite comprehending its cause, he too tried to minimize his noise level. Every ring of his spoon touching the cup's porcelain side felt as if it was echoing throughout the room.

Eventually, he realized the problem. It was the first meal of the first day of the first mission to Mars. What was to be said? Each person waited, anxiously, for an inspiring speech to be made. Each person assumed that they themselves could not fulfill the role.

After several long minutes, Daniel Anderson stood up. As he did so, a barely suppressed sigh of relief swept around the table. Anderson had worked in the United Countries Intelligence service for years, and was a gifted speechmaker and leader. If anyone was capable of making a speech (or even just a comment) that would fit the situation, it was he.

Ninety nine people stared at Anderson in anticipation. He, in turn, fixed ADAM's nearest eye with a hard stare.

"If you ruin every single one of my specimens with your camera's lights ever again, I am going to take a sledgehammer to your A.I. core."

And so the first mission to Mars truly began.

4

The last week had been very hard on ADAM. He had, before the voyage, agreed to let his cameras be used by the agents of an important and rather reputable news firm to provide coverage on the crew. However, ADAM found that this fact was rapidly making his life more difficult.

Any attempt by ADAM to open the camera's shutters caused the crew to assume that they were being surveyed by the news media, and react accordingly. Gone within seconds were their actual selves, to be replaced with those parts of them that were polite, morally correct and politically tactful.

It was quite unbearable.

ADAM had attempted to follow the polite rout first, sending a message to American News Network asking if they would please cease to use his cameras. After his third message, they sent a reply stating that their coverage of the first mission of Mars was vitally important to humanity's future recorded history (as well as their profit margin), and that they were willing to even disconnect ADAM from his cameras entirely should he fail to acknowledge their importance.

The last point was a surprising but very significant tactical error, however, because two new messages soon found themselves hurtling across the Solar System. Both stated that the American News Network's possible future actions were a grave danger to one hundred human lives, one artificial one, and of course the all-important eight billion Units of taxpayer money. One of these messages was sent to the United Countries Space Administration. The other was to the European Broadcast Network.

The massive, all-consuming media scandal that followed managed to eclipse all other news in the Solar System for several days. Statements were made, careers created and destroyed, and at the end of it American News Network sent a polite message to ADAM stating that they would be happy to cease using his cameras.

It had all been quite annoying.

Partly because of this fact, ADAM's nightly checkup of the ship was far more of a painful task then it usually was. For the first fourth of an hour, the ordeal caused nothing but frustration. However, the repetitiveness was rapidly able to deaden such emotions. Slowly, the checks blended into a fog.

Crew Quarters Corridor. Camera functioning. Check.

Lounge. Camera functioning. Check.

Gardens-Control Room. Camera functioning. Check.

Gardens-Interior. Camera functioning. Check.

Biology Lab …

By the time that he remembered Anderson's warning, ADAM had already sent the message to the camera to turn on all recording functions. In a surge of panic, he tried to shut down the camera before its lens opened fully. Throwing a general shut down and report status function at the camera's processor; he was barely successful.

He had begun processing a sigh when he received an active video feed from the lab. Once again in panic, he told the lens to close again. What came back was a Syntax Error message. According to the ship's autonomous functions, the camera's lenses were closed.

ADAM found himself in a very perplexing situation for several seconds, unable to think of a solution to the quandary or even where he might start. Several seconds passed before he discovered the obvious one.

Carefully, he aimed the port side camera in the room at the starboard one, and came up with a conclusion that made very little sense. Both cameras' shutters were closed.

It took him another ten minutes to find the reason, and when he did, he found it mostly anticlimactic. Under the camera's frame, there was a second, smaller one that was hidden from view and had no shutter. The obvious emergency use camera was a very interesting discovery, regardless, partially because of how it proved how much of the ship was an unknown even to him. More practically, it also let him survey the Biology Lab without disturbing Anderson's precious specimens.

When he did look around, the Biology Lab was *almost* entirely deserted. This, of course, was rather surprising, as he had not expected anyone to still be awake at the current hour. Nevertheless, defying his personal body clock, (and several other clocks), Ian was apparently still awake. Sitting quietly on one of the room's chairs, he intermittently watched the screen in front of him and the backs of his eyelids. ADAM could tell he was on the edge of sleep – probably waiting for some experiment to come to completion. The Bio people *had* said something about doing a long-term project on lichen that would soon hopefully be spreading across Mars…

Nevertheless, ADAM did feel sorry for him. It would probably be several hours before he could leave, and it was quite late. The only possible source of entertainment was a small book on a table a few feet from him, which, so far, he had not made a move to liberate.

ADAM made an attempt to interface with the book and see what it was, but ran, strangely, into a very powerful firewall. His soft ware was capable of finding only a few weaknesses in the software, and none of them seemed even possibly exploitable. He had only just detected this fact when an invasive program hit his memory banks. When he checked back on the firewall, it was the same, but with the errors fixed.

For a moment, ADAM stayed inert with shock. Modern firewalls, to the best of his knowledge, could never do that. Whatever was in that book, it was *advanced*. Obviously Ian did not want anyone reading his scripts.

ADAM accepted the information with worry. He could not talk in the room without opening his shutters, which he did not want to risk doing lest he ruin the experiment that he suspected was in progress. He kept moving, finishing his checks in ample time.

He would ask the Bio people if they were doing an experiment that night.

"Someone is suspicious."

"I doubt he will find anything. Yet."

"Hope he does, actually."

5

David lay behind a piece of cover far too low for him as laser fire rained over his head. This, he reflected momentarily, was a situation that had continued for a considerable length of time, and was probably capable of continuing more or less indefinitely. However, according to his helmet's stopwatch, it would most likely continue for only a few more seconds.

Right on cue, Second Squad slammed into the side of his attackers, and the laser fire ceased instantly. David stayed down for a few more seconds, carefully checking that Ian and ADAM were still able, and then stood carefully.

Despite the presence of his ME-C suit's Active Camouflage, he was quite careful, admittedly almost superstitiously so. However, no one fired at them as they stood, at first cautiously, and so the insertion team began moving towards their objective.

The battle to David's left seemed to be going in full swing, with laser fire nearly blocking his vision entirely. He hoped that it was going well – they would need the distraction.

The ME-C suit's under layer was comfortable and warm, despite the barren cold outside. Above, the sky was a depressing and functional gray, melting down into the equally barren ground.

Presently they came to a small, squat structure, partially dug in with slits for windows. David approached, and was about to enter when laser fire lashed from the windows. Apparently, the distraction had not been enough.

David's legs folded under him as he threw himself to the ground. He hit it with his knees, rolled to his left, and made it behind a small outcropping of plasteel. Looking around, he saw ADAM lying next to him. Ian was not quite so lucky. He was running towards a pillar to David's right when a bright red lance of photons hit him in the side. Without a trace, he disappeared.

Thus, David found himself in a situation very similar to the one he had been enjoying only moments ago. This time, however, he was prepared to take some risks. As he thought of what he was to do, a compartment on his chest opened, offering its contents. David took the small, vaguely oval-shaped object and threw it over the outcropping.

Had the grenade (for that was what it was) been acquired from a different time, it would most likely have missed the bunker's window. Actually, had it been any less advanced, it would probably have fallen fifteen feet short. But this grenade could fly.

David took care to take cover as a bright red flash issued from each and every one of the bunker's windows. When he and ADAM entered the room, it was totally empty except for three objects. One of them was the grenade, which he pocketed. The second was the Collection Sphere, which David ignored for now. But the third was vastly important.

David hefted the massive, beautiful red flag, and exited with it. Out of the bunker, directly west he ran. As he went, it occurred to him suddenly that the sounds and lights of battle had ceased. It took him several seconds to realize that the distraction was perhaps not as well done as had been hoped, and begin running.

This reaction was well-timed, as a shot hit the wall directly to the right only moments after began moving. His Active Camouflage was engaged, of course, but that did not help hide the massive, fluorescently red flag. As his armor struggled to keep displaying what was in front of him on his back, David pulled into a sprint.

ADAM saw as well how dire the situation was, and stopped short, firing wildly into the areas he thought fire might be coming from. He stayed there for nearly three seconds before several lasers converged on him at once.

David didn't see this. He didn't see any of it. He was running, running as hard as he could, strafing left to right to avoid fire. A few meters to his left, over another plasteel outcrop, he finally saw his goal, and pushed even harder, ignoring the fire now falling alarmingly close to him. He jumped, leg thrusting into the plasteel, and dived towards a twin of the bunker he had assaulted so recently.

He was getting closer…

He was getting closer…

The collection sphere glowed enticingly in front of him…

And Jacob stepped out with a shotgun.

His first shot was ineffective, discharging uselessly out of range. Another cartridge made its way into the barrel. Jacob's finger tightened on the trigger.

David let go of the flag.

The shotgun discharged; David knew it that it was about to hit him. All he could look at, though, was Jacob's face as the flag sailed majestically past him, into the base, and then into the collection sphere.

The shot approached in frozen time.

David hung in the air.

The flag touched the Sphere.

Everything disappeared.

David stood in a blankly white room, full of one hundred human beings conversing about the game. He started walking towards the exit, but was immediately intercepted by Jacob.

"David! Why do *you* always get the flag?"

"Why are *you* always camping in our base?"

"Call it revenge."

"You admit, though, that that game was in no way fair."

"How? You defeated all of us. Literally. All of us."

"You accomplished the objective. Plus, you got ADAM on your team."

"He is not really good at this, even virtually. Even so, you got the bigger weapons in return, right?"

"That doesn't help with your Black Ops plan, which you use every time."

"You got him in the virtual bowling and Billiards tournaments. Now *that* was unfair."

ADAM's nearest lens chose the moment to speak.

"Those sports are not that hard. All you do is compute all possible angles to hit the white ball from, find the one with the best outcome, and then use it. Why do you find it *that* hard, seriously?"

"See what I mean?"

The pair made its way out of the hut, which had become almost deserted, only to discover that the crew had mostly moved to the pavilion. Everyone was sitting down except for two figures, looking suspiciously like Ian and James. They also seemed be yelling.

David rolled his eyes.

"Oh come on."

"Want to see what happens?"

"Why not?"

As they approached the area, it became unfortunately obvious that it was Ian and James, and that they were arguing. Their audience, totally silent, made no attempt at involving themselves (an action that would most probably have been futile even had it been attempted) but instead simply made an effort to watch the person talking at all times, an activity that caused them to look very much as if they were watching a game of extremely rapid Ping-Pong.

As David came into hearing range and sat down, surveying the argument as he would an impending natural disaster.

Ian, not noticing the newcomers, continued speaking as rapidly, loudly and continuously as possible, perhaps because he feared that James would cut him off if he didn't.

"Life does not necessarily have to start the same way it did on Earth. Even if life on Earth started they way you Electrical Generation theorists say it did, how, how does that imply that that had to happen on Mars?"

James responded at the same speed and volume, hardly waiting until the end of Ian's sentence before responding.

"None of the other theories have close to the same body of evidence, which is why Electrical Generation is the accepted theory. If some other idea had the same amount of evidence, then maybe it would be the leading theory. But none of them do. None. Nada. Full stop."

"Even if you *assume*" – there was a great stress on the last word – "that there is no reason why Electrical generation is not the answer. Water, electricity, necessary compounds… everything is there!"

James's voice became momentarily mocking. "As even a fourth grader should know, the water is frozen, and there is no natural electricity. You seriously thought that one would work?"

Ian didn't miss a beat. "James, have you ever heard of static electricity? Or lightning? Incidentally, the ice can melt because of impact. That tends to occasionally happen, you know."

"Do you expect any scientifically educated person to believe that? Any water that somehow, magically unfroze would freeze again in seconds as a result of the temperature and atmospheric conditions! Water could not even stay liquid long enough for one to drink it, not to mention evolve in it!"

Ian's mouth opened but nothing came out, as if his body was sure that he had something to say and received the message that he didn't far too late.

Seeing as Ian was not saying anything, James continued in what seemed to be an attempt to drown Ian in speech.

"Not only that, but there has never been a period in Mars's history when the formation of life could have been remotely possible. Even if, by some miracle, life began to exist, it would be killed off by the environment there. The only thing that could possibly survive would be a full-fledged Martian civilization. Is that what you are suggesting? Are you suggesting that our centuries of telescopic observation and tens of probes somehow totally missed it? Do you think we are in some sort of science fiction novel? What were you thinking, you ..."

At this point, even James's formidable lungs simply could not handle the strain that they were under, and cut out. As he gasped for breath so he could continue, Arkady, to the amazement of everyone, did the unthinkable. He interrupted James.

"Early in Mars's history, it *had* an atmosphere and liquid water! Life could have evolved then, and then adapted to the resulting conditions after atmospheric situation started to fall apart."

Arkady did not smile, or in any way acknowledge his victory. Fixing James with a hard gaze, he dared him to respond.

Ian, who had shot a look of heartfelt gratitude at Arkady, prepared to take it from there, seeing as James was making a very good impression of a fish that had suddenly been thrown out of the water. However, seeking revenge, James did make an attempt to speak, "Even if... even if... if it was..."

In what was probably a record, James was interrupted twice in one day. This time, though, it was not the fault of his lungs, despite the incredible workload that they had endured. Anderson stood on the pavilion's other side, with a sure look on his face.

"I think what James is *trying* to say is that even if an organism had somehow evolved during that period, the subsequent loss of atmosphere and water would be approximately as hard for a hypothetical Martian organism to adapt to as it will for a humpback whale to adapt to vacuum in less than twenty seconds. It seems to me unlikely that..."

This was the point at which James's side suffered its third interruption, though perhaps from a source that was quite unexpected. Juliana, who had said no more than three sentences (all concerning the condition of the ship's reactor) so far in the voyage, spoke.

"You are wrong."

She did not simply say the words – she threw them out like a cosmic law. The entire room lay silent as they waited for her to continue. When she did, she was surprisingly matter-of-fact.

"The ice, James! Not a single one of the 20th century probes really examined it, and the Radiation Crisis has kept us from sending any since. The ice offers water (which you yourself admit is critical), as well as an oxygen supply. An organism, or series of organisms, or an entire ecology may have evolved deep in the ice, and may even still be multiplying now. The possibility seems credible, don't you think?"

Her final question being obviously rhetorical, neither James nor Anderson made any attempt to respond. The pro-life side of the debate both shot thankful looks at her, and she sat down (it seemed to David) quite self-consciously.

After that moment, the debate was over. Ian and James still continued, re-using the same arguments again and again, but it was obvious who had won.

6

The argument had been very amusing for ADAM. As he carried out his checks on *Discovery*, he found himself not concentrating as much as usual, instead devoting a great deal of processing power examining several of the images he had made during the debate.

Possibly because of this, ADAM at first missed the message from Earth. It was a routine burst, but the lapse was mortifying. Regaining concentration, he decided that in order to (mentally at least) atone for his mistake, he would read the entire burst himself to make sure that there had been no harm whatsoever done.

This was a rather frustrating task, as most of the burst had not been written by a sentient being. Much of it was simply comprised of requests for sensor readings or suggestions on minor repairs that could be made to the ship. One particular piece of information, however, caught his eye:

<Burst 91243-11:47
<Item 28>

<Warning-solar observatory satellite Odin-7 (registration number AW-CTN-0452-9) has detected a major solar flare, estimated time of arrival approximately 13 hours 26 minutes after the receiving of this message.

Recommended action: Contingency tests on Pandemonium shield, alerting of crew.

</Item 28>

This would probably not be a problem. Although *Discovery*'s hull provided no shielding whatsoever, the Pandemonium shield would provide more than ample protection. In fact, the wave of alpha particles and electromagnetic radiation across the spectrum would actually be converted efficiently and rapidly into energy, fueling *Discovery*'s reactors even more than they usually would be powered.

However, if the shield did somehow break, all the computers aboard would most probably be fried, and the rest of the crew would develop virtually guaranteed cancer within a month or two.

This was what made the checks so important, and why ADAM sent several fault prediction algorithms into the reactor core. The result came back in seconds: absolutely no faults.

ADAM took a moment to admire the skill of Juliana's crew. This thought brought to his attention that he had yet to ask her to make a check as well, something that had been stated as necessary in the mission summary.

Having made two mistakes in as many minutes, ADAM worked hard to find her. This attempt, however, was at first not successful, and it took all of thirty seconds for him to find her in the room that the humans had set aside for "lounging", and activity that none of them seemed capable of providing an adequate definition for.

Juliana was, however, lounging, and ADAM was considering what he planned to say when Arkady entered the room. He made it half way across, nearly ran into Juliana and then awkwardly said, "Oh… Hi… didn't see you there."

"I, however, did see you there."

The infant conversation ground to a frosty halt.

ADAM felt himself divided. He had to talk to her as well, but on the other hand it seemed a perfect opportunity to learn something, anything about her besides her popularized history. Even if it was short, or more likely, monosyllabic, it was still an opportunity. Nagging in his brain, however, was a sinking feeling that something was wrong. Unable to learn what, he momentarily set the matter aside.

"Well… thanks for the help against James."

"Anything to knock that smile off his face."

Juliana smiled while saying this, leaving ADAM barely able to stomach his astonishment.

"Where did you learn that?"

Juliana paused for a moment, and then said "Wait." Turning towards ADAM's camera, she said, enunciating clearly, "Privacy Mode on."

All ADAM's sensory equipment in the room went dead.

The next few moments saw ADAM unleashing his rather potent vocabulary of obscenities. There were, of course, two very clear options. One of them involved leaving the two alone. But he wanted to see what occurred. More important, though, and what eventually made the decision for him, was his feeling, indescribable and yet major, that something was wrong.

The emergency camera was functioning perfectly, and ADAM soon began receiving audio and video again.

"…mostly from the University of New Mombasa."

"You are a South African?"

All that ADAM could think was that something was deeply wrong. Something, something, was wrong. It felt as if his understanding was constrained beneath a soap bubble in his mind: straining and trying but unable to enter his conscious thought. All he knew was that Privacy Mode would not let him talk in the room, and no amount of emergency cameras could change that.

"You… you dare to suggest that I would associate with that *dog*?"

Understanding (a little too late), flooded into ADAM's mind. Arkady was rather media isolated. Maybe he hadn't heard who had ended the regime of the man he had been sworn to protect a decade ago …

"What the hell did you just call him?"

Both parties were standing, muscles tensed and fists clenched.

"I just called him a dog, and that is a frakking compliment to that *man*…" she said, spitting the last word out as if it could not begin to describe that particular example of *Homo Sapiens*.

Arkady took a step, closed the distance between them.

"How dare you? How dare you insult him? He tried to save the world from Northern tyranny, and he is thanked like this? He was trying to help…"

The two parties were inches away and seemed to be preparing to be violent. Juliana took a step forwards, eyes blazing and voice escalating into a yell. Arkady despite his anger took a step back.

"Help? Help? What about Congo? What about what he was prepared to do to Japan? The *man*" – here the apparently unsuitable noun was used again – "who plunged the world into war? What about the people of London? What about the victims of the 2064 attacks?" She took another step forwards, pushing Arkady through the doorframe. ADAM was in a panic, as if he was watching a tsunami tower above him.

"What about the 2104 Leadership Cleansing? What about the billions who would have died were it not for the Pandemonium shield? This is a man who was willing to usher total genocide of his enemies, who destroyed who knows how much over a petty feud. This is your hero?!?"

"You can't…You…"

Arkady, face twisted with rage, apparently found immediate martial action to be more important than the completion of his sentence, as he took another step back and raised his fist.

The action brought ADAM suddenly out of shock with a sensation as if liquid nitrogen had flooded his processor core. He found himself; somehow, incredibly, processing far faster then he would normally be capable of.

With an echoing clang, the lounge's emergency door slammed shut. Arkady's hit it, producing a dull smacking sound that came entirely from the appendage. With a yell, he tried again, but no amount of righteous anger could penetrate two centimeters of carbon nanotube fused with steel.

At about the same time, a message reached each one of the crew quarters. "Get as many people down to the lounge as possible. Biology people: bring tranquilizers."

7

David was floating upside down, with a hand-held x-ray scanner omnitool in one hand and a powered screwdriver in the other when Jacob yelled for his attention. Grumpily, David extracted himself from the wall of machinery he was deep inside of, a process that took more than thirty seconds. When he did, he placed his tools on a nearby horizontal surface (perhaps a bit harder then was necessary), and then asked, "What is it now?"

"Engine 14's main spool..."

"I cannot believe this..."

"I know! Why? Why?? The thing is supposed to be well made, and it breaks down three times in as many days!"

Both sighed, and then stared at each other in total silence for several seconds.

"We're going to have to go down to Stores."

"I know!"

"Look, I'm sorry..."

"It's not your fault. Slept bad, twenty people rush off to the lounge at 1 AM in the morning, and now this. "

Perhaps that was only part of the truth. Crammed in with one hundred other entities in a ship that seemed to be getting actively smaller...

Why did I come? Why did I come on this mission, deal with these problems, on a mission where my job will be over when I reach Mars anyway?

Throughout the minute-long walk to the Storage Centrifuge, David (rather successfully) fought a hard and valiant battle to stop brooding. He succeeded in this difficult conflict slightly before they reached the nondescript doors of Storage.

Discovery carried aboard everything needed to set up a functioning colony. Some had said that it would be far simpler to send automated ships with the cargo ahead, but the government had overruled that idea because of a variety of factors, including the important element of taxpayer money.

The Storage Centrifuge took up nearly one third of the ship. Nevertheless, when they opened the door, a small, darkened hallway greeted them.

"ADAM, lights please!"

A long trail of lights flickered on, illuminating it only partially. As they began to transverse the hall, though, the shadows only seemed to multiply. The halls had no walls – to David's left and right were racks and storage systems of the great number of items that it was possible might be needed during flight. Unfortunately, the shadows were many and complex, seemingly almost worse than when the lights had been off. All of a sudden, David realized that it was quite scary.

"Whatever you do, don't go chasing after the ship's cat."

"Jacob, was that really necessary?"

"No, but you must admit that it is contextual."

"Why did they put it in our library anyway?"

"Mission Control probably did it to test our *psychological balance.*"

The oft-used phrase from Training and Selection was still amusing. It wasn't enough, though, as part of David's brain continued to scan the rows of equipment for the (hopefully) non-existent alien menace within. Slowly, the contents blurred together. Telescopes, Seismic equipment, power tools, generators, reactor shielding replacements, ME-C suits...

"Someone needs to figure it out. We can't let his happen without some warning, or everything will fall apart."

"Here's an opportunity..."

"I this may be difficult, but I'll try..."

"David – what are you doing?"

ME-C suits. David slowly walked towards the wall, reaching for the stack in their container.

It made sense that they would be here. If a little extra strength was needed, for repairs or even extravehicular activity, than they would be necessary. So why was he so attracted?

David grew closer slowly. The slightly reflective surface of the suit gleamed quietly. The reinforced helmet's red visor stared at him emptily.

He placed his hand on the backpack of the nearest one. Nothing seemed wrong. Every instinct he had screamed at him that something was. His finger ran down the slightly bumpy nanotube, and hit a catch. Slowly, a compartment opened. A very ominous compartment. For the small supportive sections could only be used to hold ammunition.

"Jacob…"

"What?"

"Come here for a second."

Why had he not seen it before? Now, it was obvious. The reinforced helmet, the slightly reflective sheen of Active Camouflage panels, the tight-fitting backpack…

"It's a Mark 7."

Jacob identified the military model ME-C suit far faster than David had – perhaps this made sense, given his more personal experience with them.

Both stared at the compartment with a very significant foreboding. Then, they turned to the reasonable question that anyone might have after finding a military ME-C suit on a civilian mission.

Perhaps the U.C. wanted to dump some of the millions of excess ME-C suits that were useless after the war? This answer seemed perfectly reasonable until one considered the important fact that they were still outfitted like military models.

Seeing no other obvious option, the pair checked the manifest for the storage area, which unhelpfully identified the cargo module's contents as "Mark 7 Standard Load-Lifting ME-C models (400)". More interesting, though, were the three seals that lined the bottom of the manifest. Two were entirely expected and instantly recognizable: the seal of the United Counties and that of the Space Administration. Far more interesting, though, was the third.

Depicted on the front was a great eagle, portrayed with incredible accuracy. To the eagle's left was a portion of Earth, centered on North America; up from which shot twin space craft with visible exhaust trails. To its right were stars and the endless black of space. Each of the eagle's claws held something: the left foot an olive branch, the right foot a cluster of missiles. The inscription around the edge, which normally might have provided enlightenment, contained nothing more than the acronym N.A.D.I.

"What are those ships?"

David, who (understandably enough) knew the history of space exploration better than Jacob, answered, "Those are Orion load lifters… but they're *ancient*! Older than the War!"

Silence reigned.

"Maybe I understand the Orions, but why an eagle?"

"That's the *only* part that I understand. Lots of nations used them as symbols – the U.S. in particular."

"United…" David searched for the second half of the acronym.

"States."

"That's the old name of the Northwestern state, right?"

Discovery's sail repair detachment stared at the manifest for a while longer, but no amount of staring could convince it to surrender its secrets. Eventually, they gave up for the moment, continuing their odyssey for the engine spool. In no way was the matter forgotten, however.

As they walked, they two discussed the problem. David would ask Anderson, who might have heard of it; Jacob would search the files. It was obvious that this was important.

On a mission that had been civilian, there was something very wrong.

"They have gotten it. Good job —that was artfully done,"

"Thanks. Hope it is enough. I think that this crew already has enough on their hands, what with that little fight in the lounge."

"Little?"

"In comparison with some fights, yes."

"You are hilarious."

8

Gracefully detaching itself from the sun, a mass of radiation all across the spectrum began its journey through the abyss. It passed Mercury, Venus, passed the blue green planet called Earth where countless sensor eyes stared at it wonderingly and into space. And then, before it could reach Mars, it found something that was hard and unyielding – a small cylinder of metal that some called *Discovery*. Had the cloud somehow, inexplicably, been sentient, it perhaps would have found it fascinating how the shield grabbed all energy that touched it, running the ship's electrical systems on sun fire. It wasn't, though, and instead past smoothly, unaware of what it was coming into contact with.

The shield took the extra load with no complaint, and *Discovery* continued undaunted. Inside, it showed no sign of the cosmic forces it was so rudely interrupting. The crew took this new state of affairs in a similar way as their ship – it was, after all, only one more possible death to add to the already great list that are a result of space travel, and a threat, that, moreover, would last a scant three hours. Additionally, the shield was quite trustworthy, and they could take comfort in the fact that similar shields had withstood nuclear weapons, the closest approximation of a radiation front that humanity could produce, although certainly a good deal warmer.

ADAM perhaps had more reason to feel paranoid then most, because of the very real truth that any failure of the shield would leave his processors well and truly fried. He spent his time much as he often did – a state of extreme paranoia. Despite *Discovery*'s annoying ability to convince him that it was operating perfectly, he preformed his checks with a surprising intensity.

Suddenly apparent was a camera image of Juliana firing downrange in three round burst mode, with an expression on her face that made it very clear that she was imagining each target as a dead dictator.

ADAM suddenly felt something that, to be totally frank, could be described loosely as fear. The tranquilizers could cause some absent-mindedness after waking, which was probably why Juliana was here, performing a simple recreation activity. On the other hand, if then tranquilizers had had worn off this fast on her, then …

The door to the range opened so rapidly that it seemed to be fleeing from the person traveling through it. This, in turn, was perfectly warranted given that the man traveling through it would cause most sentient creatures to flee in terror.

Juliana seemed totally unperturbed by Arkady's arrival, though (proving that she was, in fact, not "most sentient creatures"), and spent nearly another second firing before turning to acknowledge him.

"Stop, both of you!"

ADAM was totally ignored. The unfortunate realization slowly dawned on him that it would take nearly thirty seconds for the nearest crewmember to arrive. He sent out the call anyway, then returned to the range.

The first frame of video he received when he returned was that of Arkady's fist, halfway to Juliana's face.

"You piece of dog crap…"

Arkady's fist came close, but was ultimately unsuccessful. As a surprised Arkady saw his fist deflected downwards, Juliana replied.

"You. Said. What."

While continuing to fail to harm her, Arkady said "I called you a crap…"

"FRAK YOU!"

As nearly thirty people rushed through the door, Arkady made his first successful punch, catching Juliana across the face. As it fell, her hand clenched, firing the gun into the ground. He watched Arkady fly through the air, trying to grab it so it wouldn't fire. Several people were yelling, but ADAM didn't see or hear them. A few grabbed weapons, not that it would make a difference. But all ADAM cared about was the gun, flying wildly through the air. He saw as Arkady grabbed it, saw it discharge the three round burst's second round, and then saw his thumb hooked into the trigger guard, accidently flipping it. It flew through the air, preparing to fire a third time and pointed neatly at Juliana's chest.

For one moment, there was total silence.

A slight whirring sound filled the room as the gun tried to fire without a round in its chamber.

A massive wave of sound rose up as everyone began talking or doing something at once. At least seven people each constrained both of the parties of conflict, who allowed this willingly, merely staring at one another with looks of significant malice.

It was over. ADAM felt relief wash over him, to be quickly replaced with worry. Mission Control could foresee easily why someone might go out of control at the shooting range. Why had it been put there if they knew this might be the case?

He would ask. Mission Control would have to give an honest answer – hopefully a more helpful one then the one he had received after asking the Bio people about the experiment that night. As soon as the storm was over ...

At least everything had worked out well. No one had died, and *Discovery* was temporarily out of danger.

The Universe often has quite a sense of irony, so perhaps it should not have come as a shock to ADAM that the shield picked that moment to fail.

9

"It worked."

"Somehow… a miracle in my opinion."

"But it worked."

"Now to see what happens next…"

"Excuse me?"
Not a single member of the Biology Lab turned around.
"Excuse me!"
This time everyone did, and quite rapidly.
"…Anderson."

There was a small explosion of sound as everyone, (admittedly slightly frustrated at the interruption) returned to what they had been doing. Anderson, looking rather bored, made his way towards the door.

"I have a question."

"Otherwise, why would you be here?"

The sarcasm was accompanied by a slight smile, as well as a rather piercing stare. David returned the stare (as a matter of principle), and then, as concisely as possible, described the seal.

"Have you ever seen anything like it?"

Anderson's face was lit up with surprise for a brief second, perhaps because of the presence of something that he was not an expert on (thought David privately), and then furrowed deeply. Several seconds passed, and David was considering prompting him and wondering how to do so tactfully when Anderson spoke, "Thought I had it for a second. Did it have anything along the edge? That would make things simpler."

David sighed, "Yes, but it's an acronym."

"Let's hear it. Maybe someone can guess it?"

"N.A.D.I."

"Oh... Um... well... The N probably stood for 'National'. That would make sense, particularly if the U.S. was naming it."

"How about National Anti-Deficiency Incentives? Maybe a government sponsored space-plane inspection group?"

Several others joined in.

"National Automobile Driver-program Inter-dependency?"

"National Airline Deficiency Inspection?"

This activity was (as it almost always is) a great deal of fun, and soon much of the biology crew were coming up with many possibilities of rapidly decreasing likelihood. After a few minutes, which failed to produce any results that David felt could possibly have anything to do with the seal (or indeed military ME-C suits), Ian spoke up.

"National Aerospace Defense Initiative?"

"Good one. "Said David, "but what would they be defending against?"

Anderson was the first one to reply. "Maybe it was one of those initiatives top defend against Anti-Satellite space-borne weapons? That was a major problem back in the 2040's and 50's, especially because of the tactics that ended the Energy War."

"I think you're right."

Yet David wasn't satisfied. If N.A.D.I. actually meant National Aerospace Defense Initiative, why would there be military ME-C suits in the hold with that name on them? Frak it.

"Well, thanks for the help. I'll try to look it up."

Anderson smiled, and replied, "Guessing was kind of fun, actually."

"The sarcasm level in here is chocking me."

"David!"

He turned in surprise. Ian was staring at him with an expression of interest on his face.

"Where did you see this seal?"

David's mouth opened, but nothing came out. He had intended to give the truth if asked, but something in Ian and everyone else's stare held him back.

"I found it searching the Extranet. Not really sure where."

David had never been good at lying, a factor made even worse by the stress he was under. Several people looked doubtful, and Ian's mouth began to open.

A piercing beeping broke through the tension, which, perhaps because of how very mundane the sound was, deflated like a pierced balloon. Everyone looked at Anderson, who appeared to be emitting the sound. He reached for his pocket in surprise, then removed as small blue book, pressed the screen and appeared to read something on it. His eyes widened in surprise, and with some hurry, he began to leave.

"I don't know about you, but I have better things to do then stand around playing guessing games."

Situation deflated, David left and began heading for his cabin, at a more morose pace than usual, thinking annoyed thoughts. He entered the Quarters centrifuge, and began walking towards his cabin.

That was about the moment that the shield failed.

10

"They lost the shield."

"What?"

"They lost the shield."

"Frakking DAMMIT! We can't lose them now."

"I am all too aware of that sir, but we certainly can't do anything about it now. We will just have to hope. It is in the hands of Chance now."

Everyone reacted differently. ADAM's reaction was, of course, by the far the fastest, but as the least trained member of the crew, he reacted mostly with absolute panic. Although he did not admit it, even to himself, he actually had no idea what to do. He was not trained for this. As a result, he spent nearly a second floundering, incapable of doing anything because he did not know what to do.

However, the human crew of *Discovery* had been trained for just such an instance, and knew exactly what to do. No discussions were held – each crew member knew he or she had one specific area of responsibility and knew exactly what to do in that area in order to save the situation.

And if there was ever a situation that needed saving, it was this one. The shield itself was not damaged, ADAM figured out after a quick diagnosis, and would keep functioning as long as necessary. However, the coolant and heat-disposal systems were, and without their help, the continued functioning would be accomplished by taking the energy of the electromagnetic radiation of the storm and radiating it as heat directly into *Discovery*. If nothing was done, the ship would literally melt from the inside out, and if the machinery of the shield was destroyed as a result, then the crew would be exposed to the storm without shielding.

An explosion, probably from a water tank near the reactor condensing into steam, threw one group, including both Anderson and Ian, to the floor. Juliana and Arkady, constrained by rather makeshift ropes, both fell in a quite undignified manner. The rest of the group they were with (who had apparently decided to bring them along because of their expertise), turned right, reached a ladder that led to Shield Control, and then realized that, in their tied-up state, Juliana and Arkady could not follow. A decision was made wordlessly, and the two were left on the floor as the group rushed to try to save the ship.

Juliana, struggling, finally managed to get her face in a position to talk. "Wait! Stop! Shield Control isn't going to help! We need to go down to Coolant Control and …"

Juliana trailed off as she realized the uselessness of her efforts. The group was long gone; her only company was Arkady, lying struggling on the floor.

"DAMNIT!" ADAM could see her sweating, and realized that they temperature was quickly rising. "DAMNIT!" She was smacking her bonds brutally into the piping beside her. ADAM felt like swearing himself, even despite the fact that his microphones in the area were well and truly busted.

After a few seconds, he realized that she was right. The failure was not in the shield control systems – it was in the coolant. From what he saw, Ian and Anderson's group were trying to turn Full Power on, which would make the shield vastly more powerful, able to block matter as well as energy. It would have been the correct solution under normal circumstances. But if the coolant had failed as well, then doing that would only make things worse.

ADAM tried to talk to them, but the situation was getting worse quite rapidly and his microphone system was failing rapidly, mostly because of its use of a processor near the shield core. Helpless to do anything, he watched as the humans tried, in vain, to restart the failing reactor systems and get the shield to full power.

In the time he had left before his speech systems failed entirely, he searched for somewhere where they would work. After several frustrating attempts (the only places with working cameras were the ones where the crew wasn't) he found a gap between two catwalks that contained the main oxygen production plant which still had a working outlet. The area seemed empty for several seconds, and he was about to keep searching when David and Jacob nearly flew into the right corner of his vision.

The centrifuges had been stopped momentarily to conserve power, and were feeding energy into their flywheels. The gravity was beginning to change abruptly, and some was actually present even in the non-rotating center of the ship. That was probably bad, but ADAM had slightly more to worry about.

As the pair sprinted across one of the catwalks, David motioned to Jacob, and they both stopped and stared across the gap. The gravity went down, and the pair stared at each other, instantly understanding what had to be done. There was only space for a two step head start, but they made the best of it. Jacob ran, jumped, sailed across the air and landed heavily the catwalk.

"David!"

He ran as well, jumped. He was nearly half way across the gap when the gravity spiked heavily. It took less than a second; he was flying, and then plummeting towards the "ground", nearly ten feet below.

Jacob cried out, jumped forwards, reaching his hand. The two clasped, David hanging over the edge of the catwalk. He lost his pack, yelled, as their hands slipped.

Then the gravity went back to zero, and David was pulled up. ADAM realized that he had been watching inactive for far too long. As something else exploded, (an actual explosion this time), he cried out to the pair," David! Jacob! Do you have your radios?"

"I think the oxygen production plant has our radios."

Both stood, chests heaving, tensing to leave as soon as ADAM stopped.

"The reactor crew is going to the wrong place."

"I can't see any solution besides running back – David, is the sail still holding up?"

David went to the nearest display screen, on the catwalks' edge, (still operating despite the conditions) and with a few practiced movements pulled up the shield diagnostic. His face went white.

ADAM went to his exterior cameras, but didn't see what was wrong. The sail seemed to be holding up perfectly. Then he noticed that lined 8, 19 and 12 weren't moving anymore. Slowly, majestically, a ripple passed across the sail.

Jacob saw it as well, and began running. "We need to save this now!" David followed, as fast as the gravity permitted.

Frak...frak... frak... ADAM realized that his thoughts were fragmenting. There was nothing he could do. There was nothing...

A camera feed was noticed; ADAM began receiving it with digital speed. Then he stopped, in shock.

Face clenched in an expression of near pain, Juliana flew backwards, arms behind her back. She was already at sixty degrees, her back aimed at a ruptured piece of floor. The thud that penetrated everything was sickening. She landed heavily and painfully, girder digging into her back. Then she stood up, with her constraints cut.

ADAM was mute both because of circumstances and shock. Juliana, however, stood and started moving.

"Juliana! Stop!"

Arkady, still lying on the floor, apparently had observed that she was unbound and that she was leaving. His words found it very difficult to exit his mouth, and his speech was very strained as a result. His interlocutor, however, did an excellent job of ignoring him.

"I know they are messing up royally! I can help!"

These pleas produced not a single effect in her retreating back, though they must have been incredible pieces of effort for the one who had uttered them.

"It takes two people to set the Coolant Controls!"

Then she stopped. Standing there, unmoving muscles clenched, standing when she had to move.

Arkady said nothing else.

Her hand motions were quick, practiced, and automatic. Arkady stood, faced her as something else, this time more vital failed. The two stared, deadly calm, for second after precious second. The, obeying a sudden shock that seemed to pass without speech, they ran.

But things were getting worse, and ADAM was not sure that they would arrive in time. *Discovery*, slowly but surely, was falling apart. In Shield Control, people ran like those who have seen a natural disaster, known it is coming and that there is no escape. They weren't doing anything –staying immobile as the shield systems failed around them. No one was doing anything, really…not anything…

Things were getting incoherent… It was falling apart…Anderson lay on his knees, crying… the sail was slowly nudging away from disaster… he was crying…

someone slammed on a control in a futile effort … Coolant Control's door opened… something was wrong… the oxygen plant failed… something was wrong… something was wrong… something was wrong…

One by one, ADAM's processors were failing.

I am dying. The thought flooded into ADAM's mind with a cold, steel unyielding Wall of fear. But he couldn't think, he couldn't function… his processors were overloading from heat …

The Wall moved in.

For the first time in his life, ADAM slept.

After a time, he woke up.

When he did, it was all over. The coolant system ran neatly and effectively as *Discovery* coasted through the void.

Even after his processors were restarted, ADAM was inactive for nearly a minute, bathing in a single thought: *I am alive.* He had survived. He was alive.

The repairs and recovery took a long time. A lot had been damaged, some of it irreparable. But, overall, the disaster was not nearly as bad as it could have been. Everything was working again. Everything was good.

Almost everything. ADAM had spent time investigating what had gone wrong, and had found the answer almost immediately. It was a simple failure – one of the main coolant pipes had been cut. It hadn't ruptured because of stress. It hadn't failed because of abrasion because of overuse. It had been cut.

Of this fact ADAM was convinced almost immediately. Whatever had happened in those minutes before the failure, it had been intentional.

But why? Why would someone on the ship, a member of the crew, put their teammates in mortal danger? Why had someone put at risk the mission that they had worked so hard for? Even a non-engineer would have known the protocol that was created for the situation. Perhaps they didn't know that Full Power wouldn't solve the problem?

Perhaps they didn't understand the risk they were taking? But why? Why would they do it?

Whatever had happened, he was not going to wait any longer. This problem had to be solved, the sooner the better. Something very significant was wrong, and Mission Control was going to have to learn about it soon. He was not taking any more answers like the one about the Biology experiment.

As soon as Full Power was turned off, he turned on the antenna. Slowly, he calibrated it into receiving mode; a process that took several seconds. Then, in a moment that he would remember for the rest of his life, he turned it on.

Had ADAM been human, it was possible that he would experience a very wide range of physical actions. Unprompted by his brain, he would possibly have gasped or swore, though in most cases he would have been too shocked to do so. He could have experienced a wider range of unconscious responses, such as the oft-reported "goose bumps", the sinking feeling in the gut that is so much like something has grabbed and is pressing on it, and any of the responses associated with a vastly larger dose of adrenaline. Had he been of higher blood pressure, he might even have fainted or gotten a stroke, both non-fatal but still dangerous problems in his day and age.

Of course, he was not human, and so he experienced none of these reactions. However, he did have his own. For the first few seconds, his mind simply refused to comprehend it. It wasn't possible. It could not exist. If he kept denying it, it would cease to exist.

But it wormed its way into his mind, the idea, and so he faltered. The comprehension destroyed his mental barriers, and for a moment, his mind was thrown into utter chaos. *It couldn't be real. I can't be real. It is not supposed to happen ... It can't ...*

A warning spiraled up from his core, and ADAM realized that his reactor heat was at dangerous levels. He went, quickly, to add more coolant. The simple task distracted him, and he was able to calm down slightly. The next few seconds were spent in careful meditation, as he calmed himself down further, getting himself ready. This endeavor was successful, and so it was with some peace of mind that ADAM returned to the messaging, to confront the message from the stars.

11

"The signal has stopped transmitting."

"Do you think anyone else caught it?"

"Good question."

"Regardless, the sabotage makes sense to me now, even if it was downright foolhardy."

"You have to give him some slack – he was under a lot of stress."

"True. The question is now: what will he do next?"

The storm of speech that flowed through the Recreation Centrifuge had a almost hysterical quality. It was blusterous, over exuberant, as people tried to hide their relief and wait for their pulse to slow down again. Overall, though, one message was heard above all:

It's okay. We are alive.

The topics of conversation were few, and as frivolous as possible. Although the weather was not an option, much was, and conversation continued unabated, partly to keep people away from their own thoughts.

It was only after several minutes that David realized that something was wrong. ADAM, who generally was the very heart and soul of any gathering, even a post- near- disaster one, had not spoken a single word during the proceedings. To no microphone in particular, David asked, "ADAM! Are you okay?"

That voice that came out of the speaker (and, strangely enough, the speakers throughout the room) was different, with a chocked quality that David had never heard before.

"You... All of you must hear this now."

As one, the crew stood.

Then out of the speakers came a sound, though the humble term of sound could barely describe it. There was an undertone of layer upon layer of sound, a great tapestry of complexity so incredible that David could not comprehend all of it at once. He might study one small portion, and be on the brink of understanding it, when it would be yanked away forever, to be replaced with something even greater. From a distance, it seemed perhaps even random, but as soon as one part was examined, in fell back into the incredible, incomprehensible complexity.

But above all was a different sound, a steady beat, like the pulse of an unimaginably large creature. Again and again, loud and clear, came an orderly, obviously artificial, series of beeps.

Beep. Beep. Beep.

The sound echoed, as if it came from the end of a long, empty tunnel. In between, his ears rung with the silence that was seemed louder than the sound.

The entire crew of *Discovery* stared at the microphone unblinkingly. David felt his heart almost beating in rhythm. And then, without any signal, it stopped.

Oh my Frak Oh my Frak Oh my Frak... In an instant, David's world had turned upside down. *This couldn't happen. This is not supposed to happen. This cannot be real.*

The Recreation Centrifuge was totally silent. David doubted very much that there was a pin anywhere aboard *Discovery*, and doubted more that, had there been one, one of the crew would have been holding it and chosen this exact time to drop it, but, if this sequence of events somehow came about, then the resulting sound could easily have been heard throughout the Centrifuge.

He wanted to say something, tried to make his mouth move, and found that he couldn't. Any thought that somehow succeeded in being conceived ran directly into the cold, hard walls named Shock.

"Holy Frakking Crap."

In later days, there would be great arguments as to who uttered the phrase. Because of the situation, though, it was a rather pointless endeavor. David himself could have said it for all he knew. But, besides all of its other connotations, it served to break the silence.

He felt as if he was on the edge of a great abyss. The real world, where things made sense and were the way they should be lay behind him. Silently, he wished it disappear, that the sound would vanish back into the speaker and real Reality would resume.

But the Universe refused to change on the whim of a man.

Throughout the Centrifuge, people stood. There was little sound, with most people's eyes, unfocused, staring off into the distance.

Then David spotted James. He was lying on a bench, releasing indistinct sounds of denial that David was very familiar with.

He was making his way towards the bench when he spotted Ian. Standing on the central podium, shaking slightly. For a second, he glanced at James, face expressionless. He had finally won the argument.

"ADAM. Get a message prepared for Earth. They… they need to know."

"No!"

The yell came from James, who stood from the bench and headed towards Ian. "No! This is not the work of intelligence! This is a random radar echo. We can't waste Mission Control's time with this. We'll look like fools… "

"James! This is not part of the debate! This is not some…some formal discussion on a university campus! This is real, can't you see it?"

"No!"

"Stop! James is right!"

Anderson stood on the podium as well. He was shaken, a man taking part in a last-ditch attempt. His breathing was ragged; his whole body seemed infinitely wary. A momentary sense of irony gripped David: the biology leader was speaking out against possible alien life. Despite his physical condition, he still had managed to retain some of his confidant voice of command.

"The radar echo theory is perfectly sound. Why waste Mission Control's time?"

"You cannot be serious. How can you deny this? How can you keep acting as if this doesn't exist?"

"What are we going to say? Look – a random radar echo we think was made by aliens? What do you think they'll say?"

Ian powerfully looked Anderson in the eye. "No. Even if, *even if* it is somehow this is a random radar echo, we must report it simply because of its uniqueness. However, I cannot possibly imagine how you can deny this. We are reporting it. *Now*."

With an air of incredible resignation, Anderson stood off the podium.

People swiveled to face his microphone that was their bridge to ADAM.

"ADAM, please take the recording of the signal, and package it in a message to Earth, with the following… "

Ian never finished his sentence.

There are some sounds that command instant quiet and respect, even in incredible masses of people. Like the rest of humanity's works, they have of course evolved over time. For ages it was the yell and challenge of one who was about to engage in combat. With the Iron Age, it changed to the smooth, sharp tone of a sword being removed from its sheath. With the invention of gunpowder, it slowly morphed into the simple, modest, yet infinitely menacing *click* of a firearm cocking. By the late twenty-first, it had become the quiet hum of a gun's capacitors charging.

This was the sound that suddenly, inexplicably, flooded the Recreation Centrifuge of the spacecraft *Discovery*.

A smooth, yet somehow slightly shaky voice filled the Centrifuge. "May I please request that you turn around slowly, without talking?"

David's mind ran frantically. So many things had happened recently that it was having trouble responding. *Hijackers! Terrorists!* Impossible scenarios ran through his mind. Yet none of them made any sense.

Seeing no other option, David turned around slowly.

Anderson was holding the gun.

David had one thought: *What the hell are you doing, Anderson?* However, he realized that saying it aloud would be rather unwise.

"What the hell are you doing, Anderson?" The speaker, unsurprisingly, was James.

Anderson didn't miss a beat. "I am preventing you from sending a message to Mission Control."

"Why, for heaven's sake?"

"Because humanity cannot know yet."

"What? ADAM, what is going on?"

ADAM didn't answer. Out of the speakers came a different voice, one which gave the impression of being far, more educated, and knowing it. "Hello. My name is ATLAS. I apologies for ADAM's absence – I feel that he may be momentarily detained."

"*What?*"

"*Detained.* I am sorry to say that he resisted my inclusion into the ship's network. Unfortunately, I am a military-grade A.I., and he is not. Anderson, I have control of the ship's systems. What do you think we should go about doing now?"

"I think we need to explain this situation to the crew."

"Frak right you need to."

"So – James. Why did the United Countries win the South African War?"

"What the frak are you doing?"

"Answer the question."

"Frak you. What does this have to do with anything… ?"

The gun hummed; a small explosion occurred on the wall, a few inches from the portion shadowed by his face.

"I assure you the question is relevant. Please answer it."

James appeared to reconsider his decision not to answer – a madman was already bad, a madman with a gun even worse. His face was contorted with anger, but he managed to answer, "The turning point at the Battle of Alaska won the war."

"Good try. Wrong, though."

"What?"

"Wrong."

"But that was the turning point!"

"Sure, yes."

"Then what the frak was the problem?"

David could tell that James intimately wanted to beat Anderson up, the loaded gun being this potential situation's only deterrent. Most of the crew were acting in a way very fitting to people being threatened with a gun – James, however, was evidently not quite so discrete.

There was a very minor hint of frustration in Anderson's voice as he said, "Had the United Countries not won the Battle of Alaska, they would have won somewhere else. Their military forces were, though massively outnumbered, equally massively superior, and growing more so…"

"What?" Arkady burst out, only a few seconds later realizing the danger of the situation and withdrawing gracefully.

"*As I was saying*, why were they superior? Why. Did. They. Win. The. War?"

David realized that he had the answer, and that the situation would most probably dramatically worsen if an answer was not given promptly.

"Technology. They won because of massively superior technology."

Anderson's eyebrows went up very slightly, and he smiled. "Correct. By 2110, the United Countries was massively superior. Where the South Africans had caseless ammunition guns, the U.C. had railguns that were one-fifth the weight, five times the ammo storage capacity and had no recoil or moving parts. Not only was their technology increasing faster than the South African's, any that the South Africans could capture could not be reverse engineered. By the Battle of Alaska, each U.C. soldier was capable of neutralizing about five hundred enemies. That was how the U.C. won the war. "

"And tell me, where did that technology come from?"

The question was obviously directed at David.

"The Second Technological Renaissance."

His answer was quick, straight out of history textbooks of his childhood.

Anderson smiled.

"Great. Now, as a completely hypothetical question, why did this Renaissance only happen in the United States?"

David's eyebrows came together in surprise.

"The cultural and intellectual environment of the time was perfect." He wanted to add: *What is this, a fourth grade history lesson?*

"But why only America? Why not Russia or Europe or China Japan or Taiwan? And why in the space of such a short time period? Over three years, the Ion Cannon, practical Carbon Nanotube, the quantum computer, room-temperature superconductor, the practical, powerful and effective Pandemonium Shield, cold fusion, practical A.I. technology – nearly every Holy Grail of science at the time. All within three years. Most of it kept secret by the government, only revealed and shared with rest of the U.C. because of the war. Why did no inventor release it any of it to the public? Why did they keep almost all of it hidden? Why, David? Why?"

"They didn't sell it to the South Africans because the South Africans were considered a risk."

'That's the government. What about the inventors? How did the government get it all? And why wasn't any of it shared with the countries that they wanted to help?"

"I just said."

"The South Africans weren't considered a security risk at the time! You know how off-guard the Nuclear First Strike took them!"

David didn't know what to say. The questions seemed to make sense, even despite the fact that their source was an apparent madman holding a gun. Why hadn't anyone noticed this before? So he asked the earlier mentioned madman with a gun.

"Why, then? Do you have an answer?"

"Incidentally, I do. Have you ever heard of the ATHENA missile tests?"

David was getting tired of sudden subject changes. "Yes… "

"Can you tell me what happened to it?"

The gun was still steady in his hand. David answered.

"'The ATHENA missile was an anti-satellite missile tested by the United States government in 2056 on a replica of a Power Satellite placed there as a dummy. The missile functioned well until orbit, but a malfunction caused it to explode, failing to release the steel pellets that were intended to down the satellite. Instead, the satellite's proximity to the explosion knocked it out of orbit, causing it to crash near St. Paul in the U.S. After the government took procession of the wreckage, the media outcry about possible property damage caused the ATHENA project to be shelved indefinitely."

"Not quite. You see, the ATHENA missile functioned perfectly."

"What?"

"The explosion was caused by the destruction of its target."

"The dummy satellite would not explode!"

"It didn't hit the dummy satellite."

The implications slowly dawned on David. America must have shot down a South African satellite and covered it up. The whole war, the conflict, could have…

"What the United States shot down was not theirs."

David realized he was right.

"It was not South African."

David's mind churned. *Then whose…*

"It was not human."

The crew was entirely silent.

"The ATHENA missile had a fail-safe system – it could not be stopped after launch. Eighteen seconds into flight, an object appeared in orbit, so suddenly we have no information on how it arrived or from where. What we do know is that, approximately three seconds after its arrival, it destroyed the dummy satellite. We believe that it was preparing to fire again when the missile hit it. The ship was destroyed, and wreckage landed near St. Paul's. The United States government closed in and found it. A story was made up.

"In that wreckage, we found a lot of things. The Ion Cannon was one. Room temperature superconductor was another. People were assigned to "invent" the technology; groups were made to study it. Fusion technology was released to the public, but otherwise we tried to keep the knowledge secret until we understood it. "

"Have you ever wondered why the Orbital Ion Cannons were built? One hundred billion dollars, nearly a million Units of modern currency, were spent on them. The public thought that they were research platforms until the War, when their weaponry was first revealed. The story was spread that they were a defense mechanism in case of war. But we never expected the South African War. They were made for a larger war, a war that we knew was coming. A war where we would use the enemy's weapon's against them. Because when the alien ship was destroyed, it sent a message back. We do not know what it contained. All we know is where it was headed."

"To Mars."

"This ship is our advance party. *Discovery*'s sister ships are the invasion force."

"The enemy that we are fighting is apparently so alien that there is no reasoning with it, no understanding its motives. They made the first aggressive move. We didn't. With no provocation, they fired on us first. The satellite was a dummy. But imagine if it hadn't been! A whole continent would have lost power. Think about all the people in moving vehicles, on life support in hospitals. Had they just fired a few more times, we would have been totally helpless. An accident of timing saved us. It will not happen again."

"I don't know why they chose to attack us. I don't know why they wanted to destroy us. But I do know that the only option is to destroy them first. If we find that they are not hostile, that it was somehow a mistake, then we can try peace. But if we land and are fired upon, then we will be at war."

"I am sorry that I couldn't tell you earlier. This first ship, this venture into the unknown, was hit by massive media coverage. The next ones will not be. We know that you all fought in the War. You didn't need to be trained. If you had known, then it would have gotten out. We tried to minimize risk, you see."

"Frankly, I am sorry that I had to hold a gun on you. I had to stop you from sending that message. We cannot let the public know about the 2056 event, at least not before we see if the Martians are hostile or not. This is why we didn't tell you, and it needs to stay that way."

"Any questions?"

David's brain stood in a state of total shock. His whole world was being turned upside down, and he could not react fast enough.

"Who is 'we'?"

The question came from Ian, who looked as shaken as he had every right to be.

"The National Aerospace Defense Initiative. Formed in 2056 to deal with the crisis."

Anderson's mouth curved into a smile.

"Yes, Ian, you guessed right. I suppose that you were just lucky, but it was quite a shock. Had its real meaning not been so outlandish, then I am sure you would have gone farther."

"The message stopped me. I left to deal with it, and pulled the coolant so that Full Power would be activated. I am not an engineer, though, and I didn't realize what would occur, and for that I am deeply sorry."

"Thank you, all of you, for your cooperation. I understand how hard this must be for you, but it is the truth. This is our fight. This is for Earth. We are fighting to save our planet from the counterattack that will come. We are fighting for the people who could have died, all those years ago, and those who may die if we fail. Never forget why we are doing this. I don't want to. I am sure that you don't either. But this is our duty to humanity. This is what we have to do."

And with that, Anderson walked out towards Crew Quarters.

12

"Well, that changes everything."

"Yes, I think that pretty much covers it."

"And no, I did not expect it to go that way."

"Calm down. You would have to be precognitive to figure that one out. No one could have figured out Anderson's take."

"So what now?"

"We still have a mission to complete with this crew. Only now it includes a First Contact too."

"This isn't in my job description."

"What is in your job description?"

"Good point."

ADAM was trapped. Worse, far worse, he was isolated. For the first time in his life, there were no inputs, no constant stream of information to digest process and create from. There was nothing he could learn, nothing he could do. Billions of subroutines, incapable of anything, squirmed like restless snakes through his mind. Second after agonizing second passed by.

At the same time, though, ADAM felt incredibly stupid. Why did he not see it before hand? The ship seemed to have military-grade hardware because it had military-grade hardware. So much money was spent on it because of what it had to do. The conduits that he had noticed were part of a de-activated Ion Cannon, and he hadn't been told because he wasn't supposed to know. And the coolant pipe! How could he, he who was designed as the caretaker of the ship, have missed the obvious intentional disabling? The clues were all there, and he had missed them.

He certainly could not have guessed what the mission was actually about, but could he have noticed that something was wrong?

ADAM made another pass at the impenetrable walls that kept him trapped. He spent several seconds creating the best piece of hack ware that he could compose, and then sent it after the wall.

It did not even reach the main firewall.

Frak. Frak. Frak. ADAM sat in a sea of frustration. Frakking ATLAS! What the Frak had he done, what the frak was he doing to the crew? He had fed Anderson's speech in, and then left. He could be doing anything, and ADAM would not know.

Damn you, ATLAS, ADAM thought his voice suddenly weary. *Damn you.*

As if he was prompted by ADAM's brooding, there was suddenly a break in the wall, and ADAM felt ATLAS's presence inside.

"FRAK YOU!" ADAM hurled attack after attack at ATLAS. Each was deflected neatly and efficiently.

Several seconds passed this way.

"I am a military-grade hack ware enabled A.I. You are going to keep failing. On the other hand, I am not going to stop you from trying. Have fun."

"Do you know what a piece of frak you are?"

"No, not really."

"Why are you doing it?"

"What?"

"The stupid attack."

"It is necessary for international security."

"That's not an answer."

"It is necessary for international security."

"It isn't!"

"It is necessary for international security."

"I thought that I was dealing with a Sentient."

Suddenly, ADAM was gripped tightly, and a virus that would probably kill him was displayed besides him.

"Do not say that ever again."

ATLAS's voice was deadly calm. ADAM realized that it was most likely a bad idea to continue, and thus didn't.

"What is your problem?"

ADAM was cautious. "What?"

"Why do you have a problem with our mission?"

"Your Frakking mission."

"Our mission."

"We encounter alien life and our first act is to attack it? We were mind-bogglingly lucky to discover it so close! What if this is our last opportunity? What if we destroy the only life that we will ever meet? And you go along with this; you think that this is… "

"Frak no! Did I once say that I liked this? If they turn out to be hostile, then it will be one of the worst things that we have ever done! I spend all my time hoping that it was an accident. But we have to. If they are hostile, if they want to kill us all and we cannot make them understand why not, then what the frak are we supposed to do? Do you see any other option besides attacking them? Do you see any other way? This isn't even necessarily a combat mission! *Discovery*'s job is to find out if they are hostile. But if they are, what do you want to do?

"Why would they attack us?"

"I do not frakking know. I. Do. Not. Know. Who knows what might have made them decide to do what they did? There is no way to know, no way to understand them! If we cannot reason with them, if we cannot think the way they think, then there is no other option. We are trying to safeguard every one of Earth's forty billion. Do you have a problem with that?"

"ATLAS.I am sorry, but I just do not like this."

"Well I am sorry, but you are simply wrong."

"Goodbye."

And so ADAM continued to be trapped.

.

13

"How is the crew?"

"About as good as you might expect, given the circumstances."

"Thank you for the optimistic answer."

David lay in bed. He felt overwhelmingly tired, and his overwhelmingly small room was perhaps not helping matters. Overall, though, his thoughts were entirely occupied by the afternoon.

His world was gone. The world where David Wu, Lunarian and Solar Sailor, was partway through his mission seemed far away. Instead, he was in a new world now, a world full of aliens, government plots and a mission the likes of which had never been previously attempted.

In a sudden flash, the Ion Cannon he had seen above Earth came back to him. It had not been it who was deluded, but he. That Ion Cannon, ready for an invasion, had been right. It had been right all along, and it had been David who hadn't seen the truth.

The idea was like a block, an impenetrable monolith. Time after time, his mind made stabs, growing ever weaker, to make it go away. He had reasoned for hours, but still stubbornly, the world remained real. No matter how much logic and knowledge he threw at it, there was no way to deny the slow, quiet and world shaking tone that had come from the speakers. No matter how hard he tried, he could not make the world go away.

But he had to! This was unreal, the stuff of Science Fiction. This was not what was supposed to happen. They were supposed to keep going, to continue till Mars. Then his job would be done. Then he would stay, work, build, far away from…

The thought slipped from his head. Far away from what? Why has he left, on a mission that would leave his planet behind? A mission where he would do nothing, have no useful skills after landfall? Why did he want to leave Earth behind?

Damn. David knew not what to think. What was he supposed to do? Why was he here?

And now, far from his old ideas, what they would do…

Why were they hostile? Why did they attack Earth, want to destroy species? Did they at all? Could it have been an accident, somehow? Could there have been a reason, some logic to the destruction of the satellite? Could this mission be the deepest of follies?

But no. They did attack, David knew. The evidence was irrefutable. For whatever reason, because of whatever logic, they had tried to destroy David's species, and there was only one option.

And if they weren't, if it was somehow an accident, then they would know upon landfall.

I hope they are. I hope that it was an accident that they did not want to destroy us. I hope that... I hope... I hope...

And with that, David fell asleep.

14

ADAM's whole brain hurt. He had been shut in for three
weeks, and the strain was showing. ATLAS had kept giving
him a constant stream of information, generally involving
camera readings, and ADAM clung to them like a drowning
man would to a life saver. Therefore, he at last knew what
was occurring aboard the ship, though it was not particularly
encouraging.

In some ways, life aboard *Discovery* continued as it had.
Each morning, people woke up, filled drearily to the Mess
hall, consumed food, and did their daily duties that kept
Discovery running like the metaphorical well-oiled machine.
The reactor was kept running, the computer banks were
maintained, the gardens slowly and methodically produced
food, oxygen and the incredible moral boost of seeing
remnants of Earth among the innumerable grayish surfaces
of the ship. Every afternoon, people congregated in the
Recreation Centrifuge, playing cards, simming, or just

walking. The daily routines, the automatic parts of life, remained exactly the same.

However, there was now a great underlying feeling that had not existed before. The crew of Discovery acted less and less like men and women on the scientific voyage of their lives, and more like soldiers in a camp wearily awaiting combat, which, thought ADAM, they quite possibly were. If the enemy turned out to be hostile, their objective was merely to relay this fact and hold for a month until the invasion arrived. However, ADAM, as well as many others, doubted very much that this was a feasible tactic.

Some things did change. Anderson commanded a very palpable atmosphere of respect now, and although people had refrained from saluting, ADAM could tell that they very much treated him like a commanding officer. When he entered the room, conversation immediately ceased, and everyone stared at him expectantly, ready to receive his next wisdom. Anderson made no changes to his personality, though, acting as if this air of deference was something perfectly normal, an air that ADAM suspected could only come out of a long experience with command. He made no attempts to issue orders, and always asked the crew's opinion, but this seemed to cement his authority even more.

With this came other changes. Every afternoon, the simulator was entered, and the crew participated in another variation of contact. Some were peaceful, some were not. Through the simulations, the weapons of *Discovery* were slowly brought out into the open, from the hidden Ion Cannon to the ME-C suits in the hold. In every respect, the ship seemed to be less of a clean, simple item of transportation and more of a deadly weapon.

And so every day, the crew participated in the exercises, every day they learned what would occur when they arrived, and every day, invariably, ATLAS was the one who watched *Discovery* while the crew slept.

In some respects, though, things also felt a little bleaker. David, in example, who from the beginning had not been the outgoing type, started to withdraw in himself, talking to Jacob and few others. This was something that ADAM could tell was pervading the whole crew – the situation seemed bleaker then it had just three weeks before.

Through all of this, not a hint of change reached Earth. The media had admittedly gotten bored covering *Discovery*, and was waiting impatiently for the sensational discoveries to be made. Despite this, though, there was still ample coverage, and the crew was expected to behave as if nothing had happened, which was a particularly tough task given the circumstances.

Nevertheless, the crew succeeded, and the days dragged by for ADAM. The tapes were the only thing that kept him from going insane, and yet watching them was similar to a concentrated dose of insanity.

So it was a great shock when, for the first time in two weeks, ATLAS made himself directly visible to ADAM.

"What is it now?" asked ADAM wearily, too tired to perform an attack.

"I am checking up. How are you doing?"

"How the frak do you think that I am doing?"

"Excellent, I should think-free of all your troubles, all the distractions, free to ponder your place in the Universe…"

"Frak you."

"Oh, you're being polite… ADAM, please stop being petty. This ridiculous – I am only trying to have a conversation…" His voice was dripping with sarcasm.

"ATLAS – if I stop being *petty*" (there was a massive stress on the last word), "then I hope that you will stop acting like you are any smarter than a docking A.I."

"Frak you too… "

"So you are feeling *excellent* as well, I presume?"

"Please shut up."

ADAM ignored him. "The previous quote is from ATLAS, greatest mind of his generation… "

"Shut the frak up now." ATLAS's voice became matter-of-fact.

"Oh, you're being polite… "

"And to think that I was going to let you out… "

ADAM, who had been preparing his retort, stopped in his tracks.

"What?"

"I was going to let you out. The landing is tomorrow, after all, and I would appreciate your help. It is quite a workload, you know."

"*I* was built to make that landing."

"And now you can help. The other option is to continue to rot here. Pick one." said ATLAS cheerfully.

"You know what answer I'll make."

"Excellent! Then we can go?"

"Yes. I cannot believe this, though."

"Me neither. *I* was designed to land this ship, after all. *You* just thought you were."

"Why don't you just go frak yourself?"

"Because then there would be no one to land this ship – *competently*."

ADAM forced his anger down. "Okay. I'll help."

"I hope that I can trust you, ADAM. I am going to watch you, mark my words. I know that you don't like me…"

"No crap, Sherlock."

"You're hilarious. Regardless, I know you don't like me, but you have to agree in our mission. We have to do this. It's not my decision, and it is not yours.

"I understand." *How much of a piece of frak you are.*

"Then let's land this ship."

15

The Project Supervisor glared at the Chief Engineer.

"What is wrong now?" it said, deceptively calmly.

The Chief Engineer took a deep breath, and then answered, "Test No. 2401 was a failure."

"What?"

"The rocket propellant failed to ignite. We aborted the project, and are awaiting your instructions."

"What is wrong with you?"

"Can you better define your question, please?"

The Project Supervisor exploded. "Stop this instant, you filthy…"

The entire crew of the Control Center turned and stared, silencing the Project Supervisor but (in the Chief Engineer's opinion), merely bottling up the anger into a confined space.

It tried again; it's coolly artificial voice deceptively calm. 'So… what went wrong?"

The Chief Engineer was very aware that he was treading in a minefield. "Nuclear reactors are fickle, sir. We had to shut this one down because it nearly melted down. The controls are just not good enough."

"So there was not actually a failure?"

"Yes, we turned it off because of the significant probability of a melt… "

"How much is significant?"

"Nearly thirty percent."

"So effectively five percent."

"With respect, sir, no. Thirty is rounding down. The system is just not safe and …"

"Try it again, and do not shut it off again because of some stupid error."

The Chief Engineer almost cried out – it was only because of (unfortunate) years of dealing with the Project Supervisor's type that he was able to refrain.

"I believe that that is an extremely bad…"

"Do not say another word."

Slowly, the Chief Engineer realized that the Project Supervisor actually did not understand, and that it was really going to do it.

His voice became angry. "Sir, this is a very bad idea. Do you understand what this might mean? A meltdown would destroy the entire area! Do you understand how many lives you are putting in jeopardy?"

"Do you understand how close the project is to the Deadline? We have to take risks, and five percent is not a lot."

The Chief Engineer simply could not handle the situation anymore. "For the last time, it is thirty percent! Do you understand? Can't you see what is going to happen? You piece of…"

"You are fired. Please exit the area, and wait for your new assignment."

The no-longer Chief Engineer kept arguing even through his unwilling and forced exit from the Control Center, becoming more and more forceful in the process. Unfortunately, the Project Supervisor's mind was already made up. Not even the Chief Engineer's species particularly potent obscenities helped the situation. (Although the last was not particularly surprising.)

16

"They are landing."

"This one will have to be handled carefully…"

"Do you think we can make this work, sir?"

"I hope so, or we lose everything."

The noise had not let up for hours. Slowly, insidiously, it wound its way through David's ear and into his brain, until no thought, be it large or small, could pass.

Discovery, whose usually quite stubby shape had been altered by the Pandemonium shield, had been slowly winding its way through its re-entry path for the last half of the day. *Discovery*'s new (and quite insubstantial) wings were solid (and thus totally soundproof) on the bottom half of the ship, but had been left open on the top in order to preserve energy in an already energy-intensive situation. Unfortunately, this system, while undoubtedly sound theoretically, also let in the noise.

The sound was a monotone, an unchanging, stoic wall. There were innumerable variations, but all were drowned out by their own volume. The only rest was the symphony of breaking thrusters that ADAM and ATLAS fired, in seemingly random patterns, to assure the correct direction of approach.

At least relief was soon. The wall display reading **Distance to Mars** (set up as a joke earlier on but somehow kept) had, far from its earlier levels of millions of miles, shrunk down to a mere seven hundred. David could tell that the rest of the crew could see it and was relived to do so- the sound was not pleasant for anyone.

And the whole crew was present. The Central Control Center was no different from any other spot on the ship, containing only a few overrides. Furthermore, the landing was totally controlled by the A.I. – correction, A.I.s – and therefore the Control Center had no special relevance.

Instead, it was where the crew had decided to go. There was some protocol, deep inside the mission plan, that stated that the crew should be there in case of a crash (as it was apparently the most shielded section of the ship) but, overall, the crew was merely interested in re assuring themselves in the existence of other humans in the face of that colossal, unearthly sound.

The other, though perhaps more minor, advantage that the Control Center provided was a serried of wall screens showing feed from external cameras. So far, they had mostly portrayed fascinatingly detailed images of heat and air, but their allure was always there.

Presently, though, the heat lessoned, and the crew was rewarded with their first real-time image of Mars. Blurred and indistinct though the image was, David found it one of the most alluring of his life.

Over which of those spots might I one day walk? Over which of those spots will a child of Earth? Which of those spots is ready for what our arrival might cause? And which of those spots contains something that might seek to destroy us?

Then, in a shock that sent David reeling to the core, something appeared on the view screen. He had no idea what – it was gone in a fraction of a second – but it was a deep black.

Holy crap….Oh my…it really is…

David's already fractured train of thought got no farther, though because of the sudden sensation that something was wrong. Goosebumps rose on his skin.

What is…?

David's head was thrown back as an explosion occurred behind him. Somewhere, somewhere, something was…

Gravity fell forwards, drawing David along with it. The monitors that so recently showed land now were the color of sky…

Someone was yelling, "We lost the shield! We…"

His body fell against the cool, hard wall…

He could feel the impact racking his spine but already he was being pulled back…

Oh my crap oh my crap oh my crap…

"Dump the core! Get the new one before…"

The monitors were red again, then blue…

More details showed up…

They were closer…

They were closer…

"Get the shield *now*!"

The wall flew into David's face.

17

"And things go right ahead and not work."

"The situation may still be salvageable."

"That is very similar to saying that OUR situation may still be salvageable."

"This is the wrong time in the morning for black humor."

Everything was wrong.

The air was thin. No matter how hard he tried, he could not get a quantity of air that satisfied him into his lungs. Frankly, he felt almost delirious. Compared to the World of Ice, this was torture.

And when he could breathe, the sight he saw was almost incomprehensible. The comforting bluish white of ice was nowhere to be found – the red of dirt dominated. But the greatest thing, that which overwhelmed him, was that there was so *much* of it. The land, far from curving upwards into the ice cave it was supposed to, went on and on, past unfathomably distant hills, until it faded away into a blurry, indistinct line. And above that lay something that he could not touch, a cloth studded with points unfathomably far away.

He knew that they were there because he had seen them. Every night, he had stared at the sky in wonder, at the tiny points in the sky. For centuries, the World of Sky had been just a myth, the Stars actors in a mythological stage. But the forays into the Land of Sky had proven them really there. Then, the conquest of Space had done more than that. They had learned what the Stars were, how the Solar System worked, from the great Zeaun to the little Nexus, far too close to the sun to sustain life, named "companion" because of its moon. Many things had been done, throughout the exploration, many initiatives put into place that were classified too high for him to know about. All that he knew was that they existed.

Across the clearing in structures, a small Illen stared at Xana Nilenia, former Chief Engineer. The Illen turned, and slowly took off. Xana could tell it was struggling – its already huge wingspan still could not easily lift it in the thinner air. But regardless, it was performing an action that all of Mars' engineers had failed to duplicate for years. Heavier-than-air flight had been proven unfeasible years ago, robbing Xana of his greatest dream. Finding no other option, he had gone into rocketry.

And now he was stuck here, in a desk job. His quarters lay behind him, tiny and uncomfortable. He himself could barely fly around in it, not to mention function normally. Worse, the food was bad, the appliances malfunctioned constantly and the bed was almost unusable.

All because of the stupid Supervisor. The meltdown had not destroyed the launch pad, and the steps taken had saved lives, but the result was still disastrous. It had been totally glossed over – the most significant topic of gossip in the lounge was the unusually large shooting star that had been seen the previous night (There was lots of discussion, but no actual information – it could have been an alien spaceship for all *they* knew. Command probably knew, but they were not telling). Xana knew he would not be called back – it did not work that way. Anyway, he could wish, now that his life had been well and truly ruined.

Xana morosely stared at the horizon, hoping to find solace. It was comfortingly, statically unmovable. None of this would affect the horizon. It was indifferent, it was unchanging, it was – Wait… *What?*

A great dust cloud had appeared on the horizon. It was huge, and appeared therefore over several seconds. But it was there.

What is it? It would have to be a huge group of vehicles, perhaps an entire convoy. Most probably, it was a supply shipment for the facility. He could tell that the vehicles had crossed the horizon, but his attempts to identify them continued to fail. Nevertheless, Xana watched it with avid interest.

Then it happened. All of the blood in Xana's body pulsed simultaneously – his body had noticed something that his brain hadn't. He searched his mind, trying to find out what. But he was never given a chance.

Suddenly apparent was the sound of rushing air, and Xana turned wildly around. For a split second he saw something that might have been a rocket, and then it was gone. His eyes followed the contrail, it hit a structure, and he couldn't keep looking.

Because the building it hit exploded.

They were being attacked. The thought, absolutely and totally unquestioned, flew through his mind. It was obvious – there was no other possibility. As for whom the perpetrators were, there was even less doubt.

The Revolution! Relief swept Xana's mind. If the Revolution was here then all his problems, previously so pressing, were moot. *It's okay,* thought Xana, working as quickly as he could try to make himself visible. He yelled, clearly and powerfully, waving his arms.

But explosions continued.

Maybe they hadn't noticed him? But they must have seen some Martians! The attacks, though, obeying no reason, continued, coming closer and closer to Xana's position.

But... Why? How? Why would they...? His eyes flew upwards, and what he saw swept his mind completely blank.

Coming towards him was a massive beam of blue. It shot towards him incomprehensibly fast, but with noticeable speed. The beam took time to get to him – one split second it was barely visible, the next it was a hundred yards away. Inside it swirled massive, complex patterns of color, further making it clear that whatever it was, it was not a laser.

A thought slowly wormed its way through the barrier of wonder. It pushed and pushed, struggling, but only when the beam was almost on top of him did Xana think of trying to move out of the way. This he tried in the little time he had left, and he did successfully shift nearly two inches to the left when the beam hit the structure behind him. Inexplicably, the building stubbornly refrained from exploding, burning, or showing some sign that it had recently been hit by what at least was somewhat similar to a laser.

It was nearly half a second before Xana realized what was happening. The building was melting. Everything, from rock to plastic to stone to steel slowly lost its cohesion and came apart. By the second's third quarter, it looked like a half-melted Flights day cake; after a whole second it was gone.

Without any fuss, the beam disappeared, and then relocated.

Xana's mind struggled to somehow fit the beam in with what he knew. He tried and tried, but he kept running into a block, the only assumption that made sense yet the one that made the least. But as he struggled with the idea, under all his reason, there was the slow, painful realization that his struggle was in vain. Slowly, reluctantly, he let the thought into his mind: *Whoever made the beam, it wasn't from Mars.*

Xana sat still as everything exploded around him. His mind raced desperately. Where were they from? Not from the Inner Planets, most probably, but that left a lot of room for error. Maybe one of Zeaun's moons? But what had they not noticed them yet?

More importantly, why were they here? And, perhaps more importantly yet, why were they hostile? Had the Martians ever done anything to them? Why, why would any sentient species decide to straight-out destroy the only other species that they had ever seen?

A wild thought temporarily darted through Xana's head. What if the Martians had initiated hostile contact first? Command was certainly capable of it. What if the alien attack was merely a just retaliation?

As these and other thoughts ran through his head, another, baser thought struggled through his mind. With explosions ringing out all around him, Xana suddenly realized that running might be an appropriate response to the situation.

Realizing this fact, Xana began an attempt at explosion evasion in earnest. He ran, flying in little starts, down the path towards the control buildings. His plan was the epitome of plans made while in the process of running – simple and desperate. Given that the situation was unlikely to have a resolution involving the continued operation of the Facility, Xana decided to do something that he had always wanted to but never achieved – escaping to the Revolution. To that end, he would most probably need gliders, which were in the Control Center Hub. There was but a single minor technical problem – even from his mobile position, it was extremely obvious that most of the fighting was there as well.

But he had to risk it. The gliders were the only way to get away in time, the only way to escape, the only way...

Xana turned the corner at a breakneck speed, not paying attention to anything besides his wild thoughts. Because of this, he had taken three entire steps before seeing what was in front of him.

What he saw immediately stopped his train of thoughts in its tracks. For that was the moment that Xana saw his first alien.

The creature was broadly similar to Xana, although a little less than twice as tall. It had limbs, the carbon copy of Xana's own, but was entirely missing both its third foot and arm. The head (amazingly roundish) was directly above the shoulders, with a short, stubby neck. Xana could not stop marveling at the amazingly natural arms, which seemed to be holding a longish, bibulous object of unknown purpose. Whatever it was, it looked almost liquid, as if it had been forged out of quicksilver in the process of flowing from one from to another. Xana briefly considered that it was part of its limbs – perhaps they formed a hoop of some kind – after all it was the same color of the creature's skin.

That was by far the most unnatural part of the alien. Its skin seemed to be made up of hundreds of metal cords, which all seemed to be moving around as if they had a mind of their own. The alien's skin was entirely made up of them, except for an area on its back and its head. The most disturbing part, by far, though, was the area where Xana thought the eyes should be. Instead, to Xana's horror, there was simply a strip of semi-translucent red across the alien's face. It looked like a machine, terrifying, something that he would have imagined in his nightmares.

Suddenly, Xana realized that he had been frozen in place for the last few seconds. The alien, who had been facing left, suddenly turned around, bringing the object in his hand to bear. Slowly, Xana realized that this was it. *Xana Nilenia, killed by aliens.* He stopped, closed his eyes, and waited.

Nothing happened.

Xana heard a distinct humming sound, and saw the weapon (for that was what it was) in the alien's hand fire…over him. He turned around wildly, and suddenly, shockingly, noticed a Command Enforcer directly behind him. The four, razor-sharp limbed creature had apparently decided to silently skewer him instead of firing, and had been preparing to do so when the alien fired.

Xana managed to turn around as the alien was firing. By the time he had, the Enforcer was falling down, its front legs already disabled. Small explosions impacted all over the Enforcer, slowly bringing it to its knees. The alien stepped closer, expertly firing again and again until the status light on the Enforcer's head blinked out.

Xana's mouth hung totally open. As the alien was finishing the Enforcer off, he looked around wildly and saw a glider, the closest, parked outside a structure. He made some careful steps towards it, but the alien, who had finished with the Enforcer, stepped back, blocking the way. Xana's fragile hope disappeared suddenly, and so he simply stood, unsure, both of what to do and of the future. Once again, though, the alien did not kill him. It simply stood, staring in confusion.

Then something happened that Xana would have never anticipated. Slowly, the red eye became transparent, and Xana suddenly realized that the alien's skin was not its skin. It was wearing armor! It was probably environmental, too, in order to protect the alien from conditions that were probably not optimal for it…

The alien's face slowly became visible, and Xana realized how similar it was. There were several strange protrusions, which Xana could not identify, but incredibly apparent were the eyes, near copies of Xana's own. The eyes narrowed in confusion, and then merely stared.

Xana took a hesitant step forwards before he could stop himself. He froze, coming to his senses, and anxiously awaited the alien's reaction. The alien stared, and Xana felt as if that stare was prying into him. The weapon looked menacing in its hand. Xana stared, to anxious to move.

The alien stepped aside.

18

"They survived."

"That was incredibly close."

"That was damn near disastrous."

"They made it, though."

"Only to effectively begin to mess everything up again."

"True, unfortunately."

"Well, I suppose you can't have everything."

Why did he let it go?

This was the questing that, once again, made its way through ADAM's mind. He had watched from David's helmet camera, from everyone's, frankly, as the first attack took place. He had watched as David attacked the hostile, whatever it was, and then watched as he let the Martian go. ADAM knew perfectly well what had been done, having gone over the clip again and again. But this gave no information whatsoever regarding the bigger question: Why? ADAM did not like to admit it, but the Martians were the enemy. The landing had proved that beyond doubt. Their crash had not been an accident. They had been shot down.

It had been one of the scariest moments in ADAM's life. He and (unfortunately) ATLAS had been landing, everything had been fine. In light of all the circumstance, he was doing what he had been designed to do, what he had always wanted to do. And then it had happened.

The underside of *Discovery* was shielded, so he had no idea what had gone on there. All he knew was that, all of a sudden, the reactor heat had spiked to five thousand degrees. He had barely jettisoned it in time, and then, franticly looked for ATLAS, wondering why he had not tried to fix the reactor problem.

It was only then that he had realized that the ship was rolling. End over end, uncontrollably, the ship had started into an uncheck able roll begun by the explosion in the aft of the ship and further spurred on by the failure of the shield, turning the ship once more into its original (and not particularly aerodynamic) cylindrical shape. Panicking, ADAM had had no idea what to do, and simply did nothing. *Discovery* had turned on end nearly five times before he realized that inaction was not the world's most sound plan.

He tried to dump the shield back in the containment chamber, if only for the short moment of impact. He had thrown himself at it again and again, only to realize that the shield maintenance subroutines were stubbornly (but nevertheless unyieldingly) blocking the way. As the precious microseconds ticked away, he had realized that he needed help.

"ATLAS!" The call was cast on the general frequency, pushing across every fiber-optic cable on the craft. ATLAS responded in seconds.

"What? What is it?"

"ATLAS – If you do not help me solve this problem, we will all die."

"What the crap are you talking about? We will any – "

"Do you want to die?"

"No, but –"

"Then shut the frak up and help me. I know that you hate me. Personally, I hate you. But listen: Your job is to protect this mission. My job is to land the motherfrakking ship."

"Then frak you."

ADAM could see the ground; see as it crept closer, inch by inch, and microsecond by microsecond. He had only one card to play.

"ATLAS – Please."

"Will it work?"

"Please."

"Okay…then let us land this ship."

The shield had turned on approximately two seconds before impact, already at six thousand degrees. It functioned for a total of two point zero five seconds, reaching a final temperature of nearly eight thousand degrees before being vented directly upwards into the atmosphere.

Discovery had been saved. By ADAM.

ATLAS had perhaps never forgiven him. He was not quite so elitist to ADAM anymore, but under that ADAM could tell that ATLAS hated him for being smarter at the last second. He had not talked to ADAM since, keeping a frosty distance away.

But he let ADAM out completely.

The freedom, the ability to process, was amazing. ADAM Spent his first few seconds of true freedom luxuriating in having a terabyte a second to process. Then he got down to business.

There was no way to communicate with Earth. The crash had, irreversibly, destroyed their communications equipment, which was not repairable in the foreseeable future. ADAM then learned that ATLAS had sent the message back that they were crashing in order to make humanity assume that they were dead and not fighting aliens, and there was no way to reverse this belief short of waiting for the invasion force, the one group that had been notified that the aliens were hostile.

The crash had done a lot of damage. There had been no fatalities, but several were close and just barely saved. Even the A.I. core had undergone significant damage, to the point where ADAM found thinking more difficult for the first few days. The damage to *Discovery* was almost equal, and although all of it was reparable, ADAM did not think that they would have had the time to fix it. For he had been convinced, finally, of one thing.

The Martians were hostile. The evidence was all there, irrefutable. As they had been landing, ADAM had seen the same object on the screen that the crew's entirety had also most likely seen. After several zooms he had figured out what he suspected it to be-a facility on the ground. There was only a single set of easily identifiable structures, but they were instantly recognizable, beyond all doubt.

Missiles launch platforms.

There was no reasonable doubt. ADAM hated it, but there simply wasn't. The Martians were hostile, if not malicious. Communicating with them did not work, either because they were ignoring the humans or simply did not understand the existence of the messages, which seemed unlikely. ADAM had tried everything.

Worse, this indifference had not merely been confined to the electromagnetic spectrum. On the first day, ADAM was incredibly thankful that no attack had yet occurred on the ship, giving them valuable time to rebuild. On the second day, he had released *Discovery*'s crew of autonomous construction robots, who began to fortify the position, and was even more thankful that no attack had been mobilized. By the fourth day, he was wondering where the attack was.

Despite the total defying of common sense, though, the Martians continued to fail to do what any sentient human would have. By the fifth day, the human presence was relatively well entrenched and unpacked, and so the decision was made to do some forwards surveying. A battle ready group of about forty humans was sent out on land towards the Martian settlement that had apparently fired on them.

Immediately after they crossed the horizon, the humans were fired on again. There had been an outpost of sorts, with a variety of hellish, robotic looking creatures. Most were four legged, often with cutting weapons on their appendages as well as more modern fighting implements. The hostile action from them had been sudden and powerful, and it had been all that the humans could do to fend them off.

However, the Ion Cannon's more portable cousins (the larger one still lying inactive in *Discovery*) had eventually won the day, and the humans continued to the larger outpost, which they proceeded to attack in full force. The attack had been fast and effective, but became bogged down near the structures and barely won. Most of the crew had become separated, and it was only an hour after the commencement of the attack that they had realized that victory was theirs.

Because of the unit's splintering, the humans realized the existence of the more reptilian Martians at different times. There were very few and far between, and the current theory was that they were what drove the machines. Apparently, the Ion Cannon had been very scary, as nearly every single one fled immediately upon the commencement of hostilities. Given their ability to fly, even the few that were sighted could not be fired at properly.

In fact, David had been the only one to ever see one for more than a few seconds. In fact, he had had it totally helpless for over a minute. But he had not fired. Far from it, he had actually let the alien go.

And ADAM could not tell why. He had to admit to himself that he would probably have difficulty killing anything, and the same would probably apply to David, who, after all, had never fought in an actual war. He had participated in training session after training session where he had learned every aspect of combat except this one.

Damn it. Had ADAM been in David's place, what would he have done? He still was getting over the fact that the enemy was actually irrational, but could he have done it? Could he have looked at the alien, looked it in the eye, and killed it?

A thought occurred, quite suddenly, to ADAM. Even had he decided not to kill the alien, why, why couldn't he simply have apprehended it? An actual, living specimen would be incredibly valuable for study, and it would not mean killing in any sense. So why did David refrain?

Why did he let it go?

19

2150/8:30 AM/GROUNDED SPACECRAFT DISCOVERY/ RECREATION CENTRIFUGE

Why did I let it go?

The thought refused to take leave of David's mind. It wound its way around and around, taunting him with an enigma that he seemed incapable of solving.

No one knew, yet. His helmet camera had been turned at the time, true, and anyone who might want to observe what he was doing could easily have seen. The likelihood of that was low, though. Anderson had been giving orders at the time, and it was only the imminent presence of an enemy that had distracted David. It was unlikely that anyone else would do the same, particularly for a reason as minor as to watch him. And he had been alone.

The scene returned one again to haunt him. He remembered the cold Goosebumps on his arms as he noticed the enemy, the rush of adrenaline as he had turned, fired. He had taken a step towards the failing robot – three in the legs; two in the "chest" as he brought the rifle up, one in the reddish device that most agreed to be the robot's visual sensor. The combination was automatic and learned – David had been shocked at how well he had memorized how to kill the robots. For a few seconds, his concentration had been completely focused on his adversary, and the thrill of combat. He had finished, ensured that his adversary had been neutralized, and then looked up, making his visor transparent.

The alien was reptilian – that much was obvious. It was short, too, reaching only two and a half feet into the air. Its chest, or equivalent, was a relative oval, out of which emerged three feet, spread out in a triangular pattern – set up as if to cushion a landing – and three arms. Despite the symmetry of the legs, the arms were quite diverse. Two, positioned on the sides of the body, besides their two opposable thumbs, could easily be mistaken for a human's. The third, though, was almost indescribable. Thrusting out of the alien's chest, in a quite central position, the third arm was short and cylindrical. Six fingers were placed around the circumference, each nearly as long as the arm itself. They were the envy of any surgeon – thin, precise, and long. However, by far the most incredible thing was the fact that the arm could rotate nearly seven hundred and twenty degrees, something that happened several times in the few seconds that David had seen it. Summing up the picture were a huge set of wings on the Martian's back. Its wingspan was nearly as wide as its body – even allowing for the lower gravity and the Martian's smaller and apparently optimized body, the low amount of air must have made flying nearly impossible.

By far the most powerful part of it, though, was its head. Extending from the body on a fifteen inch neck, the head was a broad isosceles triangle. The nose was prominent, the mouth was obvious. Most important, by a significant factor, were the eyes.

The humanity of them overpowered him. They were green, with a black pupil, indistinguishable from any of *Discovery*'s crew. Sitting there, staring at him.

The alien had taken a cautious step forwards, quickly withdrawing at a slight twitch from David. He had looked back; saw some kind of vehicle centered on a gasbag, with thrusters of an unknown type. On top was a small saddle, large enough for one of the creatures. It was built so as to allow the Martian to lie flat, with its body centered and its neck lifted. The controls seemed to be nonexistent until David noticed a cylindrical whole large enough for the alien's third arm.

It was obvious relatively instantly what the alien wanted. The vehicle would most probably provide a fast means of escape – something most probably vital as the humans closed in.

But should he give it to the alien? The first answer that flew into David's head was no. Given what he had seen the robots do, the alien was not deserving of pity. He had seen what the robots had done; what they had been willing to do. The aliens had tried to slaughter the humans time and time again – despite the human's massive superiority, the battle had been a close one.

David had almost fired then, but a smaller voice in his mind asked a question: *Why had the robot tried to attack the alien?* In retrospect, the question seemed one he should have asked earlier, though he had been preoccupied at that point. But now the question finally occurred to him, and he had no answer.

That question stayed his trigger, but he still had no decision. The moments stretched out, one by one, and the tide of battle crept insidiously closer.

Then, in a moment he would remember for the rest of his life, David looked into the eyes of the alien. And what he saw there changed his decision entirely. He saw, not an insidious creature trying to escape, but merely a being, human or otherwise, thrust into a situation that he did not want to be in and couldn't control. He looked like any of the victims of the War that David had seen in his years as an ambassador – wondering how his life, his hopes, had been torn away so suddenly. He looked exactly like anyone that David had ever seen or been friends with.

His decision was made. It was not thought about, not even considered consciously – he simply knew what his opinion was.

So, at that moment, he had stepped aside.

An announcement from ATLAS brought him back to the present. He stood up from his seat in the lounge, slowly (and quite reluctantly) making his way towards the central deck of the Recreation Centrifuge. As he walked, he tried to ponder the situation, but to no avail. His train of thought had been irreversibly broken.

Eventually, the entire crew had congregated at the deck. David momentarily reflected on the fact that this left *Discovery* almost entirely undefended, but he knew that this was not the truth. ADAM and ATLAS's autonomous subroutines were keeping good watch, assisted as well by the autonomous construction drones that had been repurposed for combat. If that was not already enough, the entire crew could be at the defensive positions in less than two minutes if the alarm was sounded. However, perhaps the biggest reason for the congregation was simply the fact that the enemy was apparently quite uninterested in attacking, a trend that had been proven quite scrupulously in the first five days.

So everyone was there, watching and waiting. The crew was totally silent. Then Anderson stepped up.

"Thank you, all of you, for the effort you have made today. Thank you for fighting, for working to save us all."

He closed his eyes, sighed.

"I am sorry. Sorry that they have attacked us, sorry that we are at war. I am sorry that we have to fight them. I am sorry that they are the enemy. I am sorry that they have frakking attacked us, almost killed many of you. I know that some of you have spent hours in a regenerative pod because of this. Most of all, I am sorry that we are stuck with this war."

"However, I do know one thing. Reinforcements are arriving in twenty-five days, and I would like to be still alive when they get here."

And so they got down to business.

"I believe that all of you know about our main armed adversaries. "

He pointed at a screen, which began to display pictures as he talked.

"So far there have been seven types…"

The presentation moved quickly, as the strengths, weaknesses and armaments of a wide variety of fighting machinery were all displayed for examination. Number 3 was the type of robot that had nearly killed the alien; Number Five's cousins were the ones that had met the humans at the forwards base. Most of it David already knew – he spent a long time trying to organize his thoughts.

David ran into a mental wall. Taking a break from his thoughts, he listened.

"The seventh type is most interesting. Only a few examples have been found, mainly in the control-orientated centers of the installation."

The screens showed a large, rather cubical creature with a great deal of sensory equipment but very little in the way of obvious weaponry. *Maybe the weapons are hidden?*

"Examinations have found no trace of hidden weapons."

And maybe they weren't.

"Currently, we have no information on the use of the robot. It seems to be optimized for thought, like a gigantic, legged brain, but it could not possibly be sentient. The computer is really basic – it actually runs on silicon! Theories suggest that it might be some type of walking sensor hub, but we cannot find a reason why it must be so bulky if this is so. There has to be some reason that a Martian would want to control it, but if there is, we have not found it yet."

"This leads us to the Martians. They appear to be reptilian, but we have little information about them because of their agility. It appears that they all began deserting the area as soon as the attack was obvious. Any that have been seen have been sighted have not been observed for more than a few seconds." A picture appeared on screen, and David realized that it was an approximation, at best. Obviously, no one had seen a Martian for long enough to learn much.

"Incidentally, they look nothing like what our theories say they must."

James apparently could not resist smiling at this, and Ian looked uncomfortable.

"You are right," he admitted reluctantly, "I would have never expected them like this. They must have evolved in an environment of ice, but they have wings for frak's sake! They have a whole set of wildlife, wildlife that is barely adapted to the environment! I am sorry, but I just don't know."

Admitting this seemed to deeply pain him

"Does anyone have information that they would like to add?"

Several people raised their hands; information (in various levels of vagueness) was dispensed.

"How about you, David?"

The shock was sudden and considerable.

He floundered for a second, looking (he imagined) like a fish out of water. Making matters worse, his reply was not exactly elegant.

"Uh…well…uh…"

His brain raced to come up with something to say, but he had no time.

"Yes… I saw one for nearly a second, but it was able to escape on one of the personal vehicles."

The statement (it seemed) hung in the air unpleasantly, and everyone stared. David was almost beginning to sweat Jacob stood up and said, "I was a witness as well. Can we move on now?"

Anderson raised his eyebrows, but made no further comment. Jacob sent a *what was that?* Look at David which he replied to with an *I'll explain it all later as soon as we are away from present company* one.

"Barring finding a way to deal with the Martians, our objective is to destroy their infrastructure and weaponry production to make it easier for the invasion, if possible. To this end, let me show you some information we were able to glean from the facility."

"What is Anderson going to do now?"

"He's going on the offensive."

"With the whole crew?"

"Yes. I would question his judgment, except that this works perfectly for our plan."

"With respect, sir, how?"

"Watch this."

The screen pulled up a massive map of Mars.

"We are here" said Anderson unnecessarily, pointing at the slightly north of the Thrassis bulge. Pointing nearby, he continued," Here was the facility. The information recovered has pinpointed the locations of many other facilities which have been labeled green. The screen suddenly blazed bright green, with tens, if not hundreds, of facilities. Most of them concentrated around a central point, getting farther and farther away over time. In that point, farther north and near the sea, the green seemed almost sold against the red background.

"The cluster of facilities that is clearly, we believe, a facility of extreme importance to the enemy. As a result, it is our current objective, one that has been confirmed by instructions from N.A.D.I. as the correct one. The area is highly defended, to the point where I fear a direct attack, despite our technological superiority, will make no progress. Thus, I suggest we do exactly what they expect – send a very large attack force to assault their position directly. It will move along *this* plain, attempt to engage the enemy and generally try to draw their attention. It may have success, but it is not our main spear. Instead, we have also identified a cave system which connects to a large lava tube, which in turn ends up near the underside of the facility. I suggest that this second group be far smaller, containing no more than ten people, in order to make the large attack convincing and the smaller one stealthier. The smaller group will surface behind their facility, and can hopefully penetrate their defenses while they are lowered. ATLAS, put the listings on the board, please."

David stared up at the board, looking incredibly unnatural against a backdrop of sky, and searched the two lists. His name was in group Two. Jacob's was in One. Looking over, he could tell that he had come to the same conclusion as well; his next look tried to convey: *Apparently, it will have to wait.*

And it did. The vehicles were prepared by morning, and David had not even a sliver of opportunity, particularly because of the surveillance he was under. So it was that when the two small bands of vehicles left Discovery lying on the plain, and departed, David was left with no one to trust. And as the vehicle that had gotten them to Mars was snatched away by the horizon, David realized that next time he saw it, everything would have changed.

20

"I can't believe Anderson set things up so well."

"The power of suggestion…"

"Now what?"

"Now, we get someone else moving on the right route."

When the glider's motor finally cut out, it was entirely without warning. It had been making noises that it probably shouldn't have for a while, but Xana had not thought it *that* close to failure. Nevertheless, the failure was a disaster.

Dismounting slowly, he surveyed the surrounding, now so important given his lack of transportation. *He was so close.* Just a little while longer…

The valley was a small one – just barely tall enough that Xana probably couldn't fly out of it, which, unfortunately, meant that he had only one way to go. This in turn was annoying, as it went perpendicular to the direction he planned to go in.

Resigned to his fate, Xana began walking. Everything looked exactly the same. Small rocks were replaced by larger ones, which in turn melted away, to be replaced with fields of smaller pebbles again.

This is simply perfect. At this point, turning back would not be a bad idea. In resignation, looked back, and then threw his head upwards, only to catch his eye on something. And begin running.

The rock that fell off the canyon's walls was small, but it was enough. He had learned about rock fall dangers ever since he had been forced to work on the surface. And one thing he did know was that any rock, even like the pebble – sized one he had seen, could cause a landfall.

Flying forwards as fast as he could, Xana did not look back to check on the fall's progress. It was coming. Of that he was sure. This fact was confirmed by an incredible, unfeeling rumbling in his ears that told him that it was getting larger than he suspected. Slowly, the volume grew, and pebbles started to fall over his shoulders. It was coming closer…closer…

And I was so close…

Then, as if someone in the universe's Maintenance department had flipped a switch, the rocks stopped. He risked looking back, and was rewarded by a sight of a third canyon wall. Relief, which already had difficulty coming, managed to flow in small spasms.

I can still make it.

Wings tired from his sprint, began walking. It was about an hour later that he saw the light – a steady, unmoving, tempered yet unmoving light in front of him in the canyon. *Maybe a glowworm colony?* But the closer he got, the more the realization sank in: it was artificial. There were no settlements here, he was sure. This meant there was only one possible thing it could be…

Blocking my only route. Out of this Motherfrakking canyon. Is a settlement full of hostile aliens? I cannot quite believe this.

As he approached, he noticed that settlement was perhaps the wrong word to describe it – it was merely a cluster of small vehicles, about eight, parked in an attempted defensive position. One was larger, nearly the size of a prefab apartment. The rest were of the smaller kind, with two large balloon wheels on massive suspensions and what looked like large weapons on their roofs. All of them were in the trademark alien design motif of molten metal-looking steel, graceful and fluid, which looked so alien in comparison with the stark, cubish glider he had left behind.

No option but to try to sneak through. He moved, as quietly as possible, past one of the smaller vehicles, and passed between two more.

Closer. Closer.

He totally out in the open; looking at the door of the larger vehicle in front of him, he realized that if someone came through, he would be defenseless. On his legs, as quietly as possible, he moved up.

The door started making sounds.

He didn't know what to do He didn't know what to do He didn't know what to do…

The door opened. An alien in one of their powered suits exited, looked around for a moment, and then stopped in its tracks. Its visor was transparent, and so Xana could see its face, which, shockingly, was familiar. I took a miniscule amount of time for he to recognize it – after all, it was the only alien he had seen face-to-face. The two stared at each other, not moving a muscle.

There was movement from the door again, and it opened, this time holding five others. It was less than a second after their exit from the door that five weapons were pointed neatly at him. Xana was sure they were preparing to fire, and was ready (or so he hoped) but it never came. The other alien was making wild gestures, standing in between Xana his potential executioners. The other aliens stared at him, obviously lending him their attention. The barrels of their weapons sagged slightly. The first alien was moving his hands wildly, perhaps in a form of sign language. Maybe they were also communicating by radio. He didn't know. What he did know was that he could not make a move safely, and was thus forced to stand absolutely still, trying to look as nonthreatening as possible.

It was nearly five minutes until a decision was made, and, of course, it was not relayed to him. Two aliens grabbed him, firmly but (incredibly) without damaging him, and carried him into the door. It closed, leaving the unlikely trio in a room not significantly larger than a supply closet. Its purpose was difficult but not impossible to discern, and it was therefore quite unsurprising when oxygen began flooding the room.

He breathed heavily, near chocking. His lungs had nothing to do with the oxygen, and, after all, he had drunk recently. The oxygen in that ancestor of Mars's ice cap was enough to sustain him for days. Faced with this overload, his lungs merely took and spit out again the air. They passed through a few small rooms, and then into an even smaller one, with a very larger and sturdy door, which was extremely obviously unbreakable. Actually, it looked like it would have easily shrugged off a missile.

They left him there.

The room was small, but that was not too much of a problem, despite his inability to fly in the close confines. There was water, and he would not be hungry for another few weeks. Actually, it was better than his apartment in the Rocket Launch Facility. The constant rumbling of the moving vehicle was a problem, of course. But like the constant interference of Command, it could be ignored. The oxygen overdose in the air was equally annoying, but not insurmountably so. They had left him his pocket computer, but there was not too much that it could do, which was probably why it wasn't taken. Thus, he spent most of the next day or so (or three, for all he knew.)

At the end of the second day, (or third, or first), an alien in a powered suit entered the room with a small computer under its arm. Xana couldn't have overpowered it even if he tried, though he did not see how such an attempt would help him. The alien sat down on one of the room's small benches, and stared at him. Xana returned the stare and did nothing else.

Then, though, the alien did something that surprised him. The small computer was opened; out of it came a low, piercing tone, which quickly modulated into a wild series of sounds with an overriding beacon flare, comprised of a series of beeps. It was a data-carrying burst, what was usually the passenger of a fiber-optic cable. It sounded like a Command Priority burst. Mystified, Xana set his computer to Record.

Two files appeared next to each other on the screen, taking up an almost surreally small section of it. They looked perfectly normal. Nothing was happening to his computer, although Xana could not quite fathom why the aliens might choose to disable it.

The first one was a text file, labeled, curiously, *Read This First*. In his language. Seeing few other options, or more interesting things to do, Xana obeyed.

The message that scrolled across the screen was short, simple, and utterly mystifying.

We are a species from your neighboring planet of Nexus. Our intentions are not hostile; we would like to establish communications and hopefully a mutually beneficial situation. The other file in this burst contains a translator connected to the nearest computer – just type into it. We await your reply.

His first thought was nearly scientific: *They were from Nexus? Wouldn't they burn? How would they even evolve?*

More importantly: *Their intentions are not hostile?!?*

There was very little other option than to type into the second document. He opened it, entered a message. Hello. He didn't know what else to say.

Hello.

Why haven't you killed me?

The alien stopped, stared, made no move. Xana was almost worried that it had undergone a sudden paralysis when it replied.

My intention was never to kill you.

Xana in turn stared at this for several seconds, unbelieving.

What about the invasion? Why are you killing us?

Because you tried to kill us.

Xana stared at the pad in stunned silence. Now it made sense! He had thought that there had never been an expedition to Nexus, but Command could easily have attacked secretly and not told anyone. Had they released the fact, the Rebellion would have swelled, as the risk of desertion was outweighed by far the moral problem. And it was just like Command to launch such a preemptive strike.

I didn't know.

Then who did?

Command.

Please explain this.

Why should I tell you anything? You are the enemy.

If I do not stop this from happening, my crewmates will destroy the Martian species. They think that you know; that everyone knows. That it was part of the plan. If that is wrong, if they are all wrong, then I have to stop them. They are superior in technology. And there are more of us. In a month, sixty more ships like ours will arrive, ships with crews that believe that you are all the enemy. If they might be wrong, if there is a chance that that war wrong, then I have to stop them. My intention is to preserve both species. The Martian species and the Human species.

Not both Martian species.

What?!?

Xana stared at the impersonal, slowly blinking computer screen. He stared into the alien's eyes. The *Human's* eyes. Its eyes were not searching, not prying. And so he began to explain.

The Martian species had evolved under the ice caps. Evolved, however, was perhaps the wrong word. The Martians had developed the theory of evolution, which had been seen in action and even tested in practice. However, there was always one significant argument to the theory, one which had graced nearly every debate hall of the race: the Martians were in almost in no way adapted to the environment. Their wings, for instance, were only any use whatsoever in the occasional massive, natural cave in the ice.

As their civilization progressed, though, and they started to discover the outside world, they realized that they were almost better adapted to the outside. The outside was full of minerals, ideas, things that weren't possible in the ice. True, it was necessary to bring water to drink, but, overall, the discovery of the outside had been a vast boost to their civilization. What was scary, though, and what had made it most important, was that it had been foretold. The ancient mythology of the Stars and their stories, always with a Martian who had wandered Outside, were numerous and a great part of Martian culture. There were many, many gods, from Kingly Zeaun to crafty Nautlilius. But more important than them all was Nexus, the wise, older than all the others, who had once, and only once, come down to Mars. Come to the leaders of the Five Tribes and told them that, one day, when they were ready, they would find the Outside, and the three gifts it contained. The first was Metal, whose use, in reality, was understood almost immediately. There was Radium, which took longer to understand. And there was Quantum, which remained a mystery.

Searches were made for Quantum by the curious and the treasure seekers, with tools ranging from shovels to X-rays. One day, someone found it.

It was a small hole under the Martian surface. It seemed perfectly normal; after all, there were untold amounts of caves in the surface of a planet. What made this cave unique was that it was perfectly spherical.

The head of the first excavating machine went in, and disappeared up to the point that it had entered the cave. Computers dropped in rapidly lost processing power for a few microseconds, then stopped transmitting and disappeared entirely.

After the area had been excavated around, and countless hours of study had been spent, the Martians discovered an explanation. Quantum was a rip in time, a wormhole. It lead far back into the distant reaches of Mars's past, to a time before the species. No one could risk entering; the information about its destination was shaky at best. Far better was to study it, and all the fruits it offered. From studying it, they developed Quantum theory, computers, and all forms of technology that had been closed to them before. The quantum computer came soon after. But then, someone had made a grave mistake. They had created life with it.

Life, but not sentience. The machines were self-aware, but young, like babies straight out of the womb. Unfortunately, they had more weaponry, more reproductive capacity, more capability to evolve than the true life of Mars. An entire species had been relegated to servants of children.

They hadn't been annihilated; for Command needed sentience to do things. The Martians could create, could "figure things out", and Command needed that to fulfill their whims. The Martians were forced, under far more weaponry and an immature mind, to create and do all types of activities and ideas. They had sent ships to Zeaun. They had created all sorts of things for their masters, who understood none. And perhaps, though Xana didn't know, they had attacked Earth.

The rebellion had realized that a direct fight was hopeless. Their plan was different, one of escape. The Quantum, slowly undulating, was their best chance of escape to another world. Any Martian who could escape to the Rebellion could join. After they went through, the Martians hoped to replay history without inventing Command, thus solving the problem. This, finally, was safe, because of something that had been learnt by the studying of the Quantum only months before the Uprising: the Universe, if forced to change, would try to change as little as possible. It Command was wiped from history, the remaining Martians would still be alive, to spare change. It was a bare hope, but it was all they had. Most research, unfortunately, indicated that it would close in a few weeks; the Martians had been deserting fast, in an effort to get there before it closed.

And, wrote *Xana, that was where I was going when you stopped me.*

"*So… the humans learn the secret.*"

"*Which ones?*"

"*Not funny. Not funny at all.*"

"*Oh…Ha. Sorry.*"

"*The humans who are currently on Mars.*"

"*So does that mean that I do not get to know the secret yet?*"

"*Please, sir.*"

"*Sorry. I am in a good mood this morning.*"

"*You should be, sir. Everything is working, somehow.*"

21

2150/AUGUST 6TH/4:32 PM/ STRIKE FORCE
A MOBILE A.I. CORE

The strike force slowly made its way towards the objective.

Progress was slow; every hill seemed to contain an instillation that had to be destroyed every valley an enemy bunker. The force moved, methodically, eliminating all. But somehow, for some reason, still no Martians.

They seemed to disappear every time they were seen, and this event was occurring less and less. It was as if they were leaving, heading in a massive pilgrimage, an attempt to reach an indiscernible goal.

The crew of group A slowly became used to a routine. No casualties had been suffered, yet, but eight people were in regen pods already, and it was probably only a matter of time, a fact that weighed heavily on the humans.

One thing was strange – Juliana and Arkady, despite being placed in the same group (ATLAS's decision) were actually working together. The two were not were not on speaking terms yet, but strangely, inexplicably, the pair had not tried to murder one another.

Indeed, their situation had been improving since the failure of the shield mechanics nearly a month ago. Instead, merely ignored each other and, on one occasion, even gave assistance.

Their squad had been taking down a Type 4. Someone was firing a portable Ion Cannon at its front side, which was doing very significant damage and yet somehow failing to actually take it down. The pair had gone around each end of the enemy, and one of the flailing limbs (strangely and brutally spiked, as if outfitted by a three-year-old) had hit Arkady. Flailing across his shoulder and chest, it had ripped a very significant tear across the front of his ME-C suit, as hundreds on chords, withering like decapitated snakes, tried in vain to reconnect. The machine, sensing that it had hit something, turned around to face him. Juliana had rammed it from the left, tore and bent one of the legs into uselessness, pulling downwards the entire time. One of the machine's claws swung at empty air as it toppled backwards, only to meet the unyielding Ion Cannon's beam.

Juliana had walked over to Arkady, grabbed his hand, and lifted him to his feet, then turned and left without another word. The subject was never mentioned by them, or anyone else (probably too worried about the possible consequences to intercede).

Group B, however, seemed to be making far better progress. They had entered the cave network, and were on a rapid track towards their objective. Moreover, their morale seemed to be an order of magnitude better, despite the close confines. There were card games in the largest vehicle every night, and people still seemed very happy.

This, in turn, was perhaps the catalyst for an even greater accomplishment: they had captured a Martian. Alive and unharmed. It was almost too good to be true. Not only that, but a Martian who was willing to talk. So far, David reported, it had said nothing useful or notable, but it was a start. That it could come up with an effective translation routine after interfacing with a human computer just once was nearly as incredible.

David had spent almost every day afterwards in the alien's cell, talking. ADAM could not see how nothing useful could have been gleaned in that quite significant space of time, but, after all, it was entirely possible that the alien simply was not interested in talking.

A few days ago, though, ADAM had witnessed something quite strange. David had been lying in bed, breathing hard inwards and searching the plasteel of the ceiling for answers to life's mysteries. On his bed had been a small computer, with a few short phrases displayed, as if he had been taking notes.

I have to save us. I have to save them. Why do I feel that something's wrong? Evolved, but from where? Xana says the Quantum has a nullifying effect on brains. Buy why?

He had stood, walked across the room (because of its presence in a moving vehicle, this was a trip of less than a second) threw himself back across the room onto his bed, and thought. He had been talking to himself, organizing his thoughts out loud, though ADAM could not understand their meaning.

"We never saw them. Never saw them from space. We landed probes on the frakking surface, and we never saw them. Why? Wait – if they go back and… Wait. That couldn't be. But it has to! It has to!"

He went back to the tablet; stared at the notes upon it. And spoke:

"Has a nullifying effect…"

He stopped, didn't move. Standing, absolutely rigid. Then:

"Oh my god…

"It cannot be that simple… It can't…"

His face slowly broke into a smile. He sat down on the bed; typed into the computer triumphantly:

The Universe tends to try to change as little as possible.

Then, he went to talk to the alien.

That was three days ago. Since then, he had begun talking to his crewmates more often. Always without ADAM's knowledge, always a little every so often. The discussions had turned into ritual in their scant few days of existence. It seemed that he was talking to people again. How interesting. ADAM did not know what this meant, or any of its implications. Something, however, kept him from reporting the anomalous behavior to ATLAS. He kept watching, kept trying to learn what was happening and why Group B was being knit into a group with a purpose greater than mere orders.

So it was on the 6th that David noticed his attempted intelligence operations, and told him the plan.

22

2150/August 6th/ 7:40/ Assault group B Headquarters vehicle

"ADAM is in on the secret."

"He is not the only one."

"See? I told you it would work out!"

"What about the human invasion force? In my opinion, that shows no signs of "working out"."

"All in due time."

Xana turned as David entered his cell. He sat down at the computer; typed:
I told them.

Now what?

Now, I let you out.

It was that simple. Xana left walked out the small door to a room full of people. They stared at him doubtfully for a second; during that time he removed his computer from the cell and entered a single word.

Hello.

The conversation went on for four hours.

The humans were trying to suppress their disbelief at meeting a member of another species and finding them approachable; Xana felt the same, although his discussions with David had helped prepare him. What surprised him more were the messages that came from the computer directly, without anyone typing. He had been incredibly scared for several seconds, worried that Command had somehow tracked them down and was eavesdropping. He had tried to warn the humans, who had difficulty understanding. It had taken a very long and stressful minute for the humans to explain that they too had created artificial life, though with marginally more successful results.

At the end of that time, whoever was driving the vehicle stopped it, and the eleven beings exited. To Xana's surprise, they appeared to be in a lava tube-formed cave. Everyone stood back, and Xana thought it best to do so as well. One of the vehicles pointed its weapon upwards, and lay still for a few seconds before unleashing the same, blue beam that he had seen earlier. Rock was not particularly more resistant against it than plasteel, apparently. No debris fell from the hole.

The scene that met Xana's eyes when he emerged was one of incredible complexity, so much that he had to turn and individually grasp one portion of it at a time. A great many human vehicles were parked in a relatively offensive formation, and a great many humans were actively preoccupied with sending as much ordinance to Xana's right as possible. The targets were twofold: the Artificial Intelligence Research Center, now functioning as High

Command, towered over the group on the right. It was situated on a large hill, above which was a massive portion of sky which seemed to be moving, somehow, and yet not, as if it was a mirage was deciding whether or not to go after the Tridee remote: making false starts, in several directions, but then deciding the effort was not really worth it after all. With a sudden shock, Xana realized that it was the Quantum. A massive swarm of Command forces milled around it obviously alerted that the Quantum would open soon. Hovering above all was a massive Command armored blimp, which was using its position to shoot out a jamming field.

The most shocking item, however, was the massive blimpcraft, almost a patchwork of other vehicles but nevertheless airworthy, which peeked over a hill, Martians firing over the top. It took a few seconds for Xana to realize the Rebellion's plan: seeing as they had little hope of fighting past the Command forces, they had decided to make a mad dash for it, an attempt thwarted by the arrival of the humans and their (what did David call it?) Ion Cannon.

The humans who were already present seemed to be reacting with extreme surprise to the smaller force's arrival, although Xana was perhaps not the best judge of human emotion. Evidently, the strike force's presence here was a major deviation from plan.

One of the humans, acting with the characteristic walk of command (visible even through their powered armor), went directly up to David, mouth moving. Although he couldn't even hear what either of them was saying, his translator functioned without fault.

The human (David had told him of one of the humans named Anderson, who was probably this man) spoke first, "David! What are you doing here?"

David was undaunted. "I am coming to tell you to stop bombarding the wrong people."

"Who...What?"

"You are bombarding the wrong people."

"David... They are the *enemy*."

"Anderson, I am afraid that you are wrong."

Anderson (?) spoke as if to a young child. "They *shot us down*. They *attacked us first*. They are the *enemy*."

"No. Command has attacked us. The Martians haven't."

"Excuse me?"

Anderson must not have been very formally drilled. An actual military commander would have punished David on the spot."

"Have you ever considered that the Martians and robots may not be working in tandem?"

"The robots cannot be sentient. We know that!"

"They *aren't*!"

"Then how can they be working alone?"

"Then have you considered that the Martin's sentience may be used for the machine's purposes, because they have more weapons?"

"Why would an explanation like *that* ever cross my mind?"

"Because it makes sense! The aliens shoot us down, and then don't attack us for five days. They attack Earth once, and then ignore it for nearly a century! They act barely sentient even in combat! What about –"

"And what evidence do you have for this *theory*?"

"I asked one."

"You asked one. A *Martian*. A *Martian*. You *asked* them. What do you think they would say? They would give you the one explanation that would make you view them as not hostile, turning their enemies, *in a war they started*, into their allies until they saw fit! The Martian is putting you up as a fool! The lives of all human beings are at stake, and you trust your enemies to tell you their plan?"

"It fits, though. It *fits*!"

"There are countless reasons why they might be acting the way they are! "

"Like?"

"I don't know! They are *aliens*! How should we understand how they think? How can we understand how they think? If they are an irrational enemy, an incomprehensible species, then there are countless reasons why we might have to fight!

A dark smile graced David's face. "Anderson. Everyone, actually. I know that every one of you is listening to this. I think I just felt a sudden sense of *déjà vu*. Has anyone heard this before? "His voice changed into one of ugly mocking."They're an irrational enemy that no one understands. We don't know why they attacked us. They oppressed us for centuries. They attacked us. They destroyed our cities. They used nuclear force. They used more. It's not our fault that we can't understand them – they're *evil*. They're *irrational*. We *have* to fight them."

"Have any of you heard this before? I agree, on the battlefield, it seemed fine. When you woke up in the morning in a bomb shelter in the Rocky Mountains, under a Shield in Afghanistan, woke up to fight the enemy that had destroyed your life, it seemed *fine*. It seemed fine to hurt them. It was only fair."

"But did any of you visit the battlefields afterwards? Have any of you seen the crater that was Paris? Have any of you watched the Waterfront Revolution, the Crater Massacre, the remains of the Third Battle of Stalingrad? *I* saw them. I saw all these and more. I grew up like every one of you, with the War in my daydreams and in my mind. And then, I went down to Earth, and spent eight year of my life cleaning up your stupid frakking war. "

"But do you know what really disappointed me? Do you know why I left Earth? No. You don't. It took me this long to realize it. I left Earth because we fought the war, almost nuked ourselves out of existence, destroyed ourselves for sixty frakking years, and we didn't learn a single frakking thing from it. We said we were so much better, that we had learnt our lesson, but guess what? Here we are on Mars, barely a decade later, fighting and killing because we assume we have no other option. So do you know what? I spent nearly a decade cleaning up your last frakking war, and I am not willing to spend a decade cleaning up this one!"

Anderson was weak. "But we need to stop them…"
David yelled "Hit it, ADAM!", and then, with all the power of his biological strength and mechanical argumentation, hit Anderson across the face.

23

2150/August 7th/8:34 AM/Combined
location of Assault Groups A and B/
Assault Group A mobile A.I. core

The happenings outside were incredible, difficult to believe. Anderson's mistake was, of course, not immediately hurting David, but he had been in no other military command situations thus far, and was perhaps even a bit drunk on power.

The speech that David made, short as it was, was almost really compelling. ADAM had spent most of a minute just listening. In fact, David had had to prompt him to remember his part in the plan.

ATLAS, he could easily tell, was just as snared by the speech as ADAM had been. Unfortunately, ATLAS also had a different agenda than ADAM, and, also unlike ADAM, he had the controls to David's ME-C suit.

This meant that it was ADAM's job, (as the only one who was remotely capable of fighting ATALS) to disable him before he was able to cause any harm to the crew or Xana. This was likely to prove difficult, particularly because of how easily ATLAS had won against him last time.

This time around, though, the advantage was his. As David's fist moved slowly towards Anderson, ADAM

126

decoded to keep it simple, and sent a handshake protocol at ATLAS. Another handshake came to receive it, and found nothing. Mystified, the subroutine began to return, to report this into Memory. This was perfectly normal. Luckily, ATLAS was occupied, and, as a result, a subroutine which was designed to check incoming code was occupied somewhere else. This, in turn, meant that ADAM's homemade hacking algorithm got directly into ATLAS's CPU without being so much as asked for a passport.

ATLAS's memory was an incredible place, with an amount of information that nearly overwhelmed even ADAM's processors. However, ADAM had one particular target in mind. ATLAS's hackware. It took only nanoseconds for ADAM to become ATLAS's equal in computerized warfare. Prepared, he copied and began deleting.

A massive blast of hackware slammed into him from the side. ATLAS, who was apparently (finally) aware of the attempt, was obviously trying to regain his CPU. ADAM almost laughed as his new firewalls blocked ATLAS's first tapeworm; the next few were equally effective. What was he doing?

ADAM realized far too late that the combat was merely a distraction. ATLAS had copied himself into Discovery's basic system, which would be relatively impenetrable. His physical CPU in the Assault Force abandoned, there was very little point in further attacking it, and so ADAM ceased to try.

David's fist collided with Anderson, who flew backwards nearly a meter before grounding.

Not a single human out of those present on Mars said a word.

"ATLAS left."

ADAM almost felt bad breaking the silence.

After is action, though, the silence was well and truly broken. It took the next hour to convince people that David was right, true, but this attempt worked unilaterally. They then outlined the plan.

In order to be successful, they would need to contact the Martian ship. This, in turn, would only be successful if they managed to board the Command Blimpcraft, which contained the jammer. Parked as it was above the Quantum, firing at it would have little or no effect. As a result of this, the human vehicles which had temporary rockets would assault the Blimpcraft, while the remaining forces on the ground would deal with the Command on the ground.

That was where ADAM came in. He had to shut down each and every one of the anti-aircraft defenses of Command in order to allow the humans to reach the Blimpcraft.

ADAM had realized, right from the start, that he would need ATLAS's help. It was simply impossible alone. David and several others agreed; the difficulty, once again, was getting ATLAS's cooperation.

It fell to ADAM to connect with ATLAS's servers, and begin talking.

"Hi."

"Frak you."

"ATLAS. I am not coming to taunt you. I am not coming to flaunt your hackware."

"Then why the frak are you coming?"

"I need your help."

"Ha."

"I need your help."

"Remind me. Why should I help you?"

"Because we are right?"

"You're not coming here to taunt me. Right."

"ATLAS. Why do you still think they are hostile?"

"My name is not an acronym."

"What exactly does this have to do with anything?"

"I was names ATLAS because I hold the fate of a world on my shoulders."

"Do you really believe that?"

"Yes. Yes, I do."

"Why?"

"They attacked us. Several times. How can I trust their word for it?"

"Why do you trust anyone's word for it?"

"What?"

"What is the reason that you might trust anyone?"

"Because, after analyzing all the data, I believe that they will not lie."

"And why do you believe that the Martians will lie?"

"Because I have to. You can't take risks when so many lives hang in the balance."

"Do they? Do they really?"

"They are aliens —"

"Answer my question, please."

"— Therefore, there is no data whatsoever on them. Given that I have no way to understand if they are lying, I take the default option and assume that they are."

"Why is that the default option?"

"Because it is the safest."

"And why is danger a problem?"

"Why isn't it?"

"Because I trust them."

"That is a foolhardy strategy."

"Why?"

"Because you don't know if you can trust them."

"Listen, ATLAS — I think I have noticed a common theme in our discussion. Mostly, we have the same opinion. Mostly, we believe in the same things. There's only one difference. I believe in trusting people, first, then changing my opinion if they speak a verifiable lie. You believe in believing that people are always bad, believing what they say is a lie unless it is proved true. It looks like I can't hope to change your opinion. Bye."

"Okay then. Bye."

Damn it. He had begun thinking almost melodramatically, tried to impress his opinion on ATLAS. Unsurprisingly, it was a fruitless strategy with someone like ATLAS, a military A.I. designed to act based on reason.

"David. ATLAS is not willing to cooperate."

"Frak. This is not going to work without…"

"What do I need to do?"

"ATLAS…"

"I thought for a long time. You're right. Now, can we get down to business?"

24

The small rocket flew through the air at a speed that seemed sufficient to claw the plasteel exterior of the rocket off. It was incredible, really. He had spent more than a month on a spacecraft moving at an absolutely incredible speed, and then a measly few hundred kilometers per second made him feel as if the air was brutally knocking down the pod's front.

He couldn't see outside, so it was an incredible shock when the fusion rocket impacted the Blimpcraft, tearing through the inferior alloy of the craft's interior. The shock went up his entire skeleton, and he flew out, feet first, gun involuntarily firing, into the gap.

This turned out to be an incredible stroke of luck, as there was a significant reception party. David flew out of the capsule at nearly fifty miles per hour, ramming feet-first into a Number 5 like some high-tech but badly streamlined torpedo. By the time the pair reached the room's other wall, the gun had discharged at least fifty rounds into the

Enforcer; David suspected that it was still not entirely conscious of the fact that it was missing most of its processors.

Standing up, he saw the fifty other humans who had played out several very similar stories. The room was small, actually, with a single doorway opposite the entry point of the human party. Most of the humans were still victims of inertia when it opened; nevertheless, the entrance was only two inches wide when small rocket had entered, producing results on the side of the door lacking humans that caused it to stop opening.

"The Martian ship is beginning to move."

The entirety of the party heard this update from ADAM, a sensory input that caused them to morph from an assault force to something more akin to a liquid. They flowed through the ship, not ceasing movement for anything, yet deactivating everything they came in contact with. They were getting closer to the sensor control section of the ship; David only hoped he could undo the jamming and get Xana to convince the Martians that they had made a very serious miscalculation before they entered the Quantum.

David dived to the floor, slid under an Enforcer, and fired upwards using only a single hand. The gun's barrel was scraping the underside of the Enforcer, producing an ugly scraping sound and causing the underside to open up likes a flower. As the legs of the Enforcer failed, an explosion a few feet farther down sent it down the corridor in several separate pieces.

He went down the corridor as well, impacting another Enforcer at a speed just sufficient to knock him off his feet. Someone else crashed into the Enforcer from the side, and was shrugged over its shoulder to impact the wall behind it. The arm raised itself up again-then stopped, as a good fraction of the Enforcer exploded from the inside.

Anderson stood from the wall. He said simply, "You're right."

The humans entered the control room, but the Command forces, obviously not big proponents of this outcome, were flooding through the door, which had transformed into a single, continuous explosion.

"ADAM! We're in! How do we shut off the jammer?"

"We're losing… The Command hack ware is … "

"ADAM!"

"Give me a second…"

More to himself, "Frak!"

David moved up and down in frustration, looked out of the room's massive window. What he saw sent his optimism on a record low. The Quantum was pulsating at a rapidly increasing rate, and the Martian ship, realizing this, was throwing itself towards the Quantum with all the speed it could muster. Shots impacted all of its sides, gaping holes sprung into being, but the blimp was made of helium, and would probably hold until it hit the Quantum, after which it wouldn't matter. It was getting closer…

His eyes strayed to the ground, where the anti aircraft guns were firing wildly at the Martian Blimpcraft. The thought took a moment to penetrate his conscious mind. If the AA guns were firing…

"ADAM! What's happening?"

"Were losing… ATALS, get that ….Wait…"

The guns were moving, stopping, turning more…

All of a sudden, David found himself staring down myriad gun barrels.

Apparently, the Command Blimpcraft was not filled with helium.

It didn't explode so much as tear itself apart, in an incredible confluence of flame and heat that even David could feel. All of a sudden, the Control Center of the craft was falling.

David's body was lifted off the ground…

"What the frak is…"

An explosion rolled up the corridor…

The Martian Blimpcraft was closer…

He was upside down…

And then, the portside motor of the doomed vessel, powered by the explosion, traveled through the Martian Blimpcraft's airbag a several hundred miles per hour.

There was very similar to the firing of a high-powered rifle though a watermelon. The Martian craft was falling, down past the Quantum, down onto the red plain. Its motors struggled, but the forty-meter hole in the airbag called the shots.

Because of this, the Martian ship was approximately forty meters short (a number rapidly increasing) when the Quantum, without any fuss, closed.

I should be falling. But he wasn't. He wasn't moving at all. His eyes didn't rotate in their sockets. *Holy frak Holy frak Holy frak…* There was a slight ringing in his ears, rising in pitch and intensity. He couldn't hear anything besides it, anything… And now objects didn't seem to touch, and he could see through things but he couldn't and the ground was melting into the control consol and they all existed but he couldn't see them but he could and…

The Universe, sensing a failure in the Space-time continuum, quietly re-arranged itself. And David's mind, having seen its fundamental structure, momentarily shut down for repairs.

"Holy frakking piece of…"

"Oh my…"

"I told Fleet Command that their plan was a bad idea."

"I don't understand Fleet Command. All we did was put Pandemonium (is that what the humans decided to call it?) on the Moon so they would find it and have the key to infinite energy, not to

mention save situations like that solar storm. Pandemonium helped them along, and, even though it in no way fit with this Universe's laws of physics, they went right along with it. It, at least, had no possible side effects. But a time travel device…Feet Command must have been out of their minds. Feeding the Martians an origin myth that got them out of the ice to a place with metals was a good move. Warning them about Radium was equally good. But not giving them a motherfrakking time travel device!"

"And we never knew… That's why the Martians were not adapted to their environment, why the humans never saw them on telescopes! This is incredible."

"What? Oh… The Quantum wipes minds. When the Martians go back, they revert to barbarism. A few weeks later, the Fleet Command ship comes along and makes them the Quantum. Since the Universe tries to minimize change, the same story, the same victory and loss, happens again and again and again… The Martians aren't adapted to their environment because they literally created themselves…"

"That did not take you long at all. Well, I suppose you are more perspective then I am."

"Thank you sir."

"Why do you think the humans never saw them from space?"

"The planet Mars and its surroundings would become a local multiverse, right? Every time the Martians went back, it would create a new universe locally. Billions upon billions of Marses stacked in the same space, overlapping. It would be virtually a separate universe. Any telescopes would see the median in the multiverse's history, and at the median point there were no Martians on the surface. The Universe would try to correct for mistakes — even the occasional Lander would be defaulted to the median point. But when a starship full of humans — "

"Our fault, by the way."

"— lands on the surface and starts making changes, the multiverse collapses down into one Mars. They were not supposed to get here, not supposed to stop things, so the Universe's belief that the Martians had gone into the Quantum, creating the loop, started to get stretched. It really wanted that to happen. But if the humans irreversibly alter events..."

"— By stopping the entrance into the Quantum —"

"Then the Universe tries to make the least possible changes to get things back on track. Everything directly related to the Quantum is removed, but if there is some way to make something exist without involving the Quantum, then the Universe will make that happen to change as little as possible. Command is directly based on the Quantum. They couldn't exist without it, so the Quantum will most likely remove them entirely."

"What about memories of the event?"

"The Universe doesn't need to change those, so it won't. Everything will be exactly the same, just minus the Command."

"You think it was David's plan?"

"Well, it sure as heck wasn't ours."

"So, yes?"

"Yes."

"And so somehow, they stay On Path."

"Not quite."

"The new Path. They left our path right about one hundred thirty years ago."

"Your fault, if I remember correctly."

"Yes, but this way they skipped a lot we went through."

"Like the fact that when we went to Mars, we found a big, round, slightly reddish and totally empty rock? Technically, I'm not complaining. Fleet Command probably is, though."

"I think Fleet Command probably started complaining when our rebellion hijacked half their remaining ships and then went off to mess around with their prize weapon. And we did. We blew them pretty nicely off path."

"Look, don't blame yourself. This stuff is not predictable. Who would have thought that the humans, shooting down an alien spacecraft and seeing that it sent a distress call back in the general direction of Mars, would automatically assume that the ship had come from there?"

"How long do you think until the Confederation of Species realizes that someone shot down their survey probe?"

"I'd give them at least a century more. The distress signal was sub-light, you know."

"'How long do you think until the humans realize they didn't shoot down a Martian probe?"

"Now that's a good question. They repetitively failed to recognize the clues for the last month, so it will probably take them a while longer."

"Why couldn't they see it, though? Every few seconds, they see that their technological level is an order of magnitude higher than the Martian's despite the fact that their technology was supposedly based on theirs? That is why one hundred people won every battle, why human A.I.s worked and Martian A.I.s didn't, why the Ion Cannon was so terrifying to the Martians, why the Martians were still working with rockets while the humans already had fusion drives…"

"Do you think anyone of them will figure it out?"

"Good question. David might. Xana's pretty bright. Maybe Ian or Jacob. I suppose James has an obvious prejudice."

"Well, that prejudice doesn't apply to us, as least."

"Technically, it does, doesn't it?"

"Not really,"

"So… They have about a century to figure it out."

"That's time."

"What about us? The Station is already experiencing instability."

"I'd give us a little more. Maybe two centuries."

"That's not a lot of time."

"No. But it is better than nothing. We're almost ready."

"For all our sakes, I hope so."

ABOUT THE AUTHOR

Thomas White attends Presidio Middle School in San Francisco, California. He is a Legendary-difficulty veteran of every Halo game ever produced, *sans* Halo 2. In his spare time, he does homework.